Pushing the Bear

After the Trail of Tears

American Indian Literature and Critical Studies Series
Timothy B. Powell and Melinda Smith Mulkin,
General Editors

ALSO BY DIANE GLANCY

Novels

The Reason for Crows: A Story of Kateri Tekakwitha
Stone Heart: A Novel of Sacajawea
The Mask Maker
Designs of the Night Sky
The Man Who Heard the Land
Fuller Man
The Closets of Heaven
Flutie
Pushing the Bear: A Novel of the Trail of Tears
The Only Piece of Furniture in the House

SHORT STORIES

The Dance Partner: Stories of the Ghost Dance
The Voice That Was in Travel
Monkey Secret
Firesticks
Trigger Dance

Essays

In-between Places
The Cold-and-Hunger Dance
The West Pole
Claiming Breath

Poetry

Asylum in the Grasslands
Rooms: New and Selected Poems
Primer of the Obsolete
The Shadow's Horse
The Stones for a Pillow
The Relief of America
(Ado)ration
Boom Town
Lone Dog's Winter Count
Iron Woman
Offering
One Age in a Dream

Drama

American Gypsy
War Cries

Pushing the Bear

After the Trail of Tears

Diane Glancy

University of Oklahoma Press : Norman

Pushing the Bear: After the Trail of Tears is Volume 54 in the American Indian Literature and Critical Studies Series.

Library of Congress Cataloging-in-Publication Data

Glancy, Diane.
    Pushing the bear : after the Trail of Tears / Diane Glancy.
        p.   cm.—(American Indian literature and critical studies series ;
v. 54)
    Includes bibliographical references.
    ISBN 978-0-8061-4069-8 (pbk. : alk. paper)
    1. Cherokee Indians—Fiction. 2. Cherokee Indians—Relocation—
Fiction. 3. Fort Gibson (Okla.)—Fiction. 4. Frontier and pioneer
life—Indian Territory—Fiction. 5. Indian Territory—Fiction. I. Title.
    PS3557.L294P88 2009
    813'.54—dc22

                                                                            2009000127

The paper in this book meets the guidelines for permanence and durability of the Committee on Production Guidelines for Book Longevity of the Council on Library Resources, Inc. ∞

1 2 3 4 5 6 7 8 9 10

At first there was nothing. There was the faint cold steady rain. The gray and constant light of the late November dawn with the voices of the hounds converging somewhere in it and towards them.

"The Old People," Go Down Moses, *William Faulkner*

We know where we're going and where we came from.
    Between two nighttimes, lightning.
And there, in that short light, a face, a strange look,
more of a grimace, lit up by the light of a death rattle.

"Between Two Nighttimes, Lightning,"
Vincente Aleisandre, translated by Lewis Hyde

Contents

Characters

Maritole
Knobowtee
Beulah, Rebekah, Willard, and Watson, their orphan
  children

O-ga-na-ya, Knobowtee's brother
Aneh, Knobowtee and O-ga-na-ya's sister
Edward, Aneh's husband

Tanner, Maritole's brother
Luthy, Tanner's wife
Mark, Ephum, Annohee, and Thomas, their children,
  and Evelene, an orphan

Reverend Jesse Bushyhead, a Cherokee minister who
  led one of the detachments
Reverend Evan Jones, a white Baptist minister who
  led one of the detachments

Anna Sco-so-tah
Quaty Lewis
War Club

The Conjurers

Pushing the Bear

After the Trail of Tears

Prologue

Resettlement

From October 1838 through February 1839 some eleven to thirteen thousand Cherokees walked nine hundred miles in bitter cold from the Southeast to Indian Territory. One-fourth died or disappeared along the way.

At the end of the removal trail, the Cherokees arrived at Fort Gibson. It was a walled enclosure that reminded them of the stockades in the Southeast from which they had come. They did not enter the fort but camped around it.

Something large was there— something in their way— as if it was a bear they could not see. They did not understand. Something had happened— a shift from everything they had known. They would have to rebuild in the new territory with what they could remember, but it too had shifted. Something else was in the way— a new weight came against them. They had to remove that also. They felt they were in darkness, though it was daylight so bright they wanted to close their eyes and cover their faces with their hands.

They had arrived in the new territory—dirty, ragged, stripped.

On March 19, 1839, Reverend Jesse Bushyhead, a Cherokee converted to Christianity, wrote a letter to the Baptist Mission Board in Nashville reviewing the removal trail.

The detachment, which was placed under my charge, left the old nation for the west on the fifth of October last, and we landed at the place of our destination on the 23rd of February. We were detained one month on the road at the Mississippi by the ice. There were 82 deaths in the detachment while on the road. There were 66 members of the church in the Baptist connection in the detachment. Out of this number, we selected two brethren to keep up regular worship during our travel; to wit, Tsusuwala and Foster who has lately joined the Baptist Church. They frequently held prayer meeting and exhorted the brethren on evenings during the week and on the Lord's day, except when the weather would not admit of it; for we rested every Lord's day, except that one time we traveled five miles to get forage for our teams.

Bushyhead's detachment had gone from Fort Cass, Tennessee, near the Georgia-Tennessee border, northwest through Nashville, across southwestern Kentucky, through southern Illinois, across the Mississippi River. They continued west across Missouri, then southwest in Arkansas to Fayetteville and west into Indian Territory, which later would become Oklahoma. They arrived at Park Hill, I.T., on February 23, 1839.

The trail, with the sick and the old and the suffering, never left his thoughts. Nor his diminishing detachment.

Sometimes in his dreams, he saw the fires they had built along the roads at short intervals to keep from freezing.

Remember walking. Remember the clouds walking with us. Remember the wind that walked with us. The cold. Remember the longing to stop marching. We have done that now. Remember the people we left in graves. Remember the voices that came from the sky. There is change. Change. Remember we knew that change was here. Remember the birds. Their voices came with us. Not the same birds, no, but the song of their voices. Remember the sound of wagons. The snort of horses. The protest of the land— not to us, no, but to the ones who made us walk. Remember the moon. Remember the corn. We will taste it again. Remember the need to listen, to hear, to live. Remember the sun that will cross the sky, that will plow the day again. Remember all things that will work again. The stars that will turn again. The cabins that will stand again. Remember the hills in the old territory that disappeared in the distance. Are they still there, far away? Yes, Thomas and others who fled there are with them.

Chapter One

Several thousand survived the march. At night, the families camped together at Fort Gibson, Indian Territory. Some of the Cherokees stayed in their detachments, sleeping under wagons. Others were in tents and lean-tos in the woods. Some slept under a cover of leaves. Their hair was dull and matted as the ground where they slept. Their clothes were torn. They were dirty. Their hands were infected with splinters, scratches, and wounds of every kind. Their skin was chapped and raw. Their faces, hollow. Their limbs, weak. Their eyes stared to the ground. They were a string of bones, some more animal-like than human.

Reverend Jesse Bushyhead and his family stayed in one of the tents the fort provided. He sat outside as he read his Bible, preparing for his sermon in the new territory. His wife was inside, feeding the baby. Reverend Bushyhead finished his study with Genesis 5:24: Enoch walked with God until he was no more. Bushyhead closed his Bible. Why hadn't he been removed like Enoch? He had walked with God on the long removal trail, yet he survived the march. He was in Indian Territory to begin again. Why was he left? Why wasn't he one who perished on the trail? He had a wife, a daughter, and a young baby. But so had others who died. He lost his sister on the trail. He lost many in his congregation, nearly a fourth. Some of them had survived to begin another journey, maybe harder than the one they had just completed. They did not have energy to begin again as yet. They sat dazed, overspent. They could not leave Fort Gibson to find the land they wanted to farm. Building a church was uppermost in Bushyhead's mind. He urged the men to build the church first. It would be a place to keep the orphans. It would be a place to stay until they got their cabins built.

"Here are the children without parents," Reverend Bushyhead announced at the service. He and his wife had rounded them up into a group. "Those of you building cabins, make room for more than your own children. We will have more in our families than we know. Widows. Men too old to build."

"*Wapump*," War Club grumbled.

Reverend Bushyhead held his church meeting under the open sky. Evan Jones and other white ministers who had walked the trail with the Cherokees joined them. Bushyhead gave thanks to God for their survival. He called men together to cut down trees for logs to build the church.

"Can God furnish a table in the wilderness? Can he give bread also? Psalm 78:19–20." Reverend Bushyhead overpreached, trying to pump faith into the people. "If there is a God, and he is who he said he is, then there will be a way to rebuild."

"I need a place of refuge," Maritole said, as she persuaded Knobowtee to help with the church.

The men brought axes from the fort. They traveled an old road until Reverend Bushyhead found the place to build the church. They cut a path into the underbrush. Dried leaves matted the ground. The woods were thick with trees on the last edge of winter. Everything was brown, but a few buds had begun to stand up on the branches like wounds. Everything was on the verge of change. Just give it a few warm days—just turn the sun on the desolate branches.

The men continued to work their way into the dense woods. They cut logs. They notched the logs for dovetail joints and lifted one log on top of the other. The women prepared the mortar. The men chiseled flat stones for the chimney. They unloaded the roof beam from the wagon. It had traveled overland with them from the old territory. The beam contained the journey. The men felt it as they lifted it from the wagon. The new, cut timber was changed by it. The old and the new had come together.

Some of the older men told how they had built cabins in the old territory. It was something some of them knew how to do, but others were hardly old enough to have learned. They had lived in cabins already built. The men worked together with Reverend Bushyhead, Knobowtee and his brother, O-ga-na-ya, Knobowtee's brother-in-law, Tanner, Evan Jones, the white minister who had led a detachment, mixed-bloods, black men, the white, War Club, Wah-ke-cha, and the other Cherokee men.

In the first service, they remembered those who died on the trail: Anna Sco-so-tah remembered Kin-chow, her neighbor. Maritole remembered her parents and the baby. When she saw Knobowtee's sister, Aneh, crying, Maritole remembered Knobowtee's mother. She remembered the Widow Teehee, Kee-un-e-ca, Mrs. Young Turkey, and those they left behind. She heard the other voices converge with names of lost relatives and friends. It was a long trail of voices that called the dead to their destination. Everyone they remembered was called to the end of the removal trail.

The War Department promised subsistence for a year after their arrival. But government contractors decided to make a profit and gave the Cherokees inferior meat and flour. Fort Gibson would provide plows, rifles, axes, oxen, horses, mules. Who knew what quality they would be? The men hunted game, deer, squirrel. They were given provisions to set up tents and temporary shelters. They had meetings. Knobowtee called many of them. His wife, Maritole, sat in the background near his sister, Aneh, his sister-in-law, Luthy, and Anna Sco-so-tah, Quaty Lewis, and the other women. Maritole was pale, thin, and discouraged as she held two small orphans. But who wasn't discouraged? They had survived. But for what? That thought now was settling in on them. They had farmed land already broken into fields. Now they would begin again from nothing in the wilderness.

"We need cornmeal if we are to have strength to begin again," Knobowtee said, looking at the flour rations at the fort, but the agent turned away.

Some of the Cherokees who began looking for land to farm came back to Fort Gibson furious. They found Creeks, Osage, and Old Settler Cherokees on the land allotted to them.

The Old Settlers had migrated to the new territory after the 1817 treaty. They didn't want to hear about missionaries and schools. They wanted to keep their traditional ways. They had migrated west to land that belonged to the Osage with whom they had fought. Maritole remembered her father had not wanted to recognize the western band of Old Settlers. Now his family would be among the western Cherokees.

The Creeks had made treaties in 1826 and 1827, giving up their land in Georgia. Some of them had settled in the new territory inside land assigned to the Cherokees by an 1828 treaty. Now there were skirmishes between the tribes— murders, burnings, spells, curses. The rain in gray sheets fell heavy, then sprinkled, then fell hard again. The people moved from rivulets that ran across the ground and threatened their camping places. They stepped through wide streams across the roads. The Cherokees sat inside under tarps, in tents, in half-built cabins. They walked through mud. It was hard enough to come to a new land, even harder when that new land was held by others.

There were more open threats. Fearing an escalation in the uproar over the land, the officials at Fort Gibson summoned someone from Washington. The United States held a council of Creeks and Cherokees at Fort Gibson to settle land rights. The Creeks had to move to the south and west of the Cherokees in Indian Territory. Then there were the white settlers, already in Arkansas. How long before they entered Indian Territory and took that land too?

Knobowtee knew there were other meetings going on, important meetings with important leaders of which he was not a part. "We have not come to unoccupied land," Knobowtee said. "The Old Settler Cherokees have been here for twenty years. They have established their lives. Maybe some of their connection to the land will come to us."

"Or we will learn it on our own," Maritole said.

Knobowtee and O-ga-na-ya stayed near Fort Gibson until the disputes were settled, fearing they would have to move again. Maritole's brother and sister-in-law, Tanner and Luthy, and their boys stayed near the fort also.

"Let's go," Maritole insisted. "Others will be farming before we get started." But Knobowtee would not move, even after the meetings that settled ownership.

When the Creeks left Cherokee land, the Cherokees rushed to the farms abandoned by the Creeks. But Knobowtee and O-ga-na-ya wanted to start over on land that had not belonged to someone else.

"I feel sometimes we have walked to the moon," Maritole said.

"There is nothing but work lined up for the rest of our lives," O-ga-na-ya said. "We won't make a dent."

"We all will plow fields," Knobowtee said. "We will hold them in common."

"There already is talk of taking care of the field nearest to the cabins we will build," O-ga-na-ya said.

"There's no land big enough for a communal field," Anna Sco-so-tah said. "It's all wooded. Not enough land has been cleared."

"We'll start our small fields and clear more trees to join them," Knobowtee offered.

"At least we won't have the militia burning our crop," O-ga-na-ya finished.

Chapter Two

It took a while for them to realize the march was over. They woke in the gray dawn with a start. It was time to get up and march. They had no strength, but they would walk another day. Then they realized they were in the new territory. They were there. They looked at the canopy of trees above them. The new leaves would bud. They looked at the open sky. They had to readjust once again. This time it was to *not walking*. This time it was the question of what they would do now. They were disoriented. At first the sounds were the same. A baby's cry. A conjurer working a spell. Reverend Bushyhead's prayer to the dawn. A cough. A stirring of those who had been asleep. But to what purpose? The journey was over. What did that mean? What would they do? Build a fire? Cook bacon? Long for corn mush? Was there a chicken nearby? Where were the orders for the day? The directions?

Maritole saw Knobowtee and O-ga-na-ya talking. Why didn't Knobowtee talk to her? Why weren't they talking about what should be done? No, Knobowtee and O-ga-na-ya were arguing. O-ga-na-ya was angry.

He was trying to persuade Knobowtee to join him. She knew that some of the men planned revenge against the three chiefs who had signed away the Cherokee lands. She knew the men met in groups to talk. Maritole turned to Beulah and Rebekah, the two orphan girls. One of them was whimpering. It was Beulah. Maritole used her blanket to cover them under their blanket from the morning air. They had dreamed they were walking. They dreamed they were in a strange land and there was nothing of comfort. They dreamed of their lost families. But Maritole could not get them to say what had happened to separate them from their parents. They were too young. They were too battered from the trail.

The Cherokees had always been divided— the white peace towns from the red war towns. No— divided wasn't the word. They were two parts of the same way of life. Settlement and defense of the settlement. It had been that way in history. But disagreement was still a part of the Cherokees. Maybe the word was division after all. The Cherokees were now divided west from east. There were divisions within the divisions. Knobowtee from O-ga-na-ya. Rebuilding and revenge. Those were the divisions between them. Men were divided from women. Men were divided from themselves. Everyone was divided from their land.

The old territory had been noisy with birds and animals, but the Cherokees had grown accustomed to it. The noise in the new territory was new. They heard the call of birds and the click of squirrels and small rodents during the day. They heard the birds with their different calls of an evening. *Chewery chewery chew. To it To it.* There were calls and answers. Twitters, gnawings, and honks. All were talking, but none were listening. All were telling their stories— the frogs at the creek, the ducks, the whippoorwills, the owl, all of them, woven together. And over that, the stars and moon with their different shapes. There were fewer trees in the new territory, though it also was wooded. Some of the Cherokees camped in the open field near the fort. It was as if the sky were upon them. It was their cover instead of the thick blanket of leaves they had known in the old territory.

The night air was cold and clammy. They also heard people coughing. They heard people near death.

Some nights as they camped under the open sky, Knobowtee tried to pull his wife toward him, but Maritole resisted.

"I'm angry because you left me to myself. I don't have someone like O-ga-na-ya to talk to. My mother died hardly before the trail started. I don't have a cabin."

"You have Anna Sco-so-tah. You have Luthy," Knobowtee said. "If you talk much louder, you'll have O-ga-na-ya to talk to. We'll get a cabin built before the summer is over."

"Then we'll have him in the loft."

"We'll get his cabin built. It takes time, Maritole. I see your impatience has survived the trail."

Maritole listened to the conjurers who told stories in the evenings as they camped around Fort Gibson. They were singing a bear-hunting song. They were hungry. There were reports of bears in the new territory— black bears. Brown bears. Maritole knew the bear stories. Bears were nearly human. They could talk. Once a hunter heard a bear singing to her cub in words he could understand.

She listened to the conjurers again.

He-e! Ani'-Tsa'guhi, Ani'-Tsa'guhi, akwandu'li
e'lanti' ginun'ti,
Ani'-Tsa'guhi, Ani'-Tsa'guhi, akwandu'li e'lanti'
ginun'ti-Yu!
I want to lay you low on the ground. I want to lay
you low on the ground.

Maybe the songs of the conjurers would quiet the people. Often Maritole felt a wave come over the camp. She felt they were tinder ready to ignite.

How could they stop the dream of walking? How could they stop the hunger? It was the stories they told. Maybe they had the old power.

At night, Maritole held the orphan girls as she sat next to Anna Sco-so-tah and Knobowtee and O-ga-na-ya's sister, Aneh, and listened to the Bear-man story around the campfire.

"At one time, food was scarce. A hunter went into the woods where two bears told him about a country where there were chestnuts, acorns, and blackberries. The hunter went to that country and lived in a cave with a bear all winter. 'Your people down in the settlement are getting ready to hunt me,' the bear said. 'They will kill me and take you home with them. When they kill me, they will drag me outside the cave and cut me to pieces. You must cover my blood with the leaves and when they are taking you away, look back and you will see something.' Soon they heard the hunters coming up the mountain. The dogs found the cave and began barking. The hunters killed the bear with their arrows. They dragged him outside the cave and skinned his body and cut him into pieces they could carry back to their settlement. The dogs kept barking and the hunters thought there must be another bear in the cave. But they saw the hunter they had been looking for all winter, and they welcomed him back with them. Then each man took a load of bear meat. Before they left, the man piled leaves over the spot where they had cut up the bear. When they had gone a little way, the man looked back and saw the bear rise out of the leaves, shake himself, and go back into the woods."

That was a story for the Cherokees. They would rise from leaves.

But there was more to the story.

"When the hunters neared their settlement, the man told the hunters he must be shut up where no one could see him without anything to eat or drink for seven days, until the bear nature left him and he became like a man again. They shut him up alone and tried to keep still about it, but his family heard. His wife came looking for him. She begged every day until, after four or five days, the hunters told her where he was. She took him home with her, but he died shortly after, because he still had a bear's nature and could not live like man."

The Cherokees were in the new territory. They could build their cabins. They could find their way. How long before the old territory left them? How long before their old nature turned to a new nature?

"I saw a small bear in the woods," someone said in the dark. Perhaps the hunters would return with a bear. Perhaps they would have bear meat to eat.

"Sometimes I want both of us go off together," O-ga-na-ya told Knobowtee. "We can start over again."

Knobowtee shook his head. "There are times you look at your wife and you don't know her. You wonder where she came from. How you ended up with her. Then you remember a girl at the Green Corn dance. You saw her hair and eyes. You wanted to talk to her. To be with her. You try to find that again."

"You won't find anything after the trail," O-ga-na-ya said to Knobowtee.

"I have to look at Maritole as someone I didn't know before. I have to take her hand and bring her to the edge of this clearing and build a cabin for her and shoot a turkey and clear a place for a garden, and soon I'll forget she's a stranger that I had chosen somehow. I'll forget she looked at another on the trail. I'll forget all her sins. Maybe she will forgive mine."

"How could we start off together?" O-ga-na-ya asked. "We would have disagreement over sin. What is it? You have a definition for a word I don't recognize."

"I forgive her wrongs. Maybe she forgives mine," Knobowtee said.

Chapter Three

"I hear chopping all through the woods," Anna-Sco-so-tah said as they followed a creek under a bright sun to scout the surrounding land for a field and a place to build a cabin.

"They left the orphans, Beulah and Rebekah, at the church. It would be too hard to carry them through the entanglement of the woods. Beulah was sick. Rebekah coughed also. Maritole asked Aneh, Knobowtee, and O-ga-na-ya's sister to stay with them. Anna Sco-so-tah would have stayed at the church, but they wanted her to help them find a place.

"Look at the way the water bends," O-ga-na-ya said. "It will flood in a downpour. The flattened weeds there— maybe a year ago."

"It will be a place to fish," Knobowtee commented.

"Keep going," Anna Sco-so-tah said.

"That clearing is too rocky."

"The soil everywhere has rocks buried in it. I can hear them."

"There to the east," Knobowtee said. "Another clearing— "

"A partial clearing," Maritole said. She felt the warm sun on her back. At least she was no longer cold.

"I want to feel my old plow handle in my hand. I want the cabin. The fields."

"Who is planting our fields now?" O-ga-na-ya asked.

"We can't think about it, O-ga-na-ya," Knobowtee said. "Bitterness is a weight we don't have strength to carry."

"They were with us on the trail— " Anna Sco-so-tah said, "the spirits. The old ones. They camped around us. They stood in the rain. They shivered with us. But they pushed the wagons. They pulled the oxen."

"I didn't see them," O-ga-na-ya confronted her.

"They have come to the new territory— Indian Territory," Anna insisted. "They are discouraged also to think of the work ahead."

"Should we comfort the dead ones?" O-ga-na-ya asked. "Should we carry the spirits? It would be hard to lift them— beings without bodies. Where is an arm? A leg? A head?"

"They calmed the horses," Anna Sco-so-tah said. "They caused the birds to sing with our songs. They talked with the voice of birds."

Knobowtee looked into the trees. The birds were wild with song. They were building nests. O-ga-na-ya, Anna, and Maritole stood quietly as Knobowtee watched, thinking he saw a sign, thinking he would know from the birds which way to turn into the woods. But the birds did not seem helpful. They did not like the intruders. They were all fussing at the group.

"We hear what the birds say," Anna Sco-so-tah said.

"Walk. Walk. Keep out of our woods," O-ga-na-ya interrupted Anna Sco-so-tah.

"No, they tell us to chop trees for a cabin. They tell us to plow."

"They tell us what to do in the darkness of our new day."

"They do not speak when the sun is gone," Knobowtee told his wife. "That's the trouble of depending on the birds."

"One night a bird called out," Maritole said.

"I heard it too," Anna Sco-so-tah agreed.

"It was a spirit in agony," O-ga-na-ya said.

"I don't think spirits feel agony," Knobowtee refuted.

"They feel our despondence," Anna Sco-so-tah said. "Not their own."

"Where do we build a cabin, Anna Sco-so-tah?" Knobowtee asked. "In the old days it was the women who knew. I have other things to do than wander in the woods."

"What have you got more important than building our cabin?" Maritole questioned him.

"I want to work on our new constitution."

"I want revenge," O-ga-na-ya said.

"Are the seeds still in your pocket?" Maritole asked Knobowtee.

"I have them. We can't plant the field yet. We don't have a field. We have to clear the land. We'll start with a garden. Then we'll build a cabin and clear a field. By then it may be winter again." Knobowtee saw that his words discouraged Maritole. She thought they would be resettled in a short time. "I think our clearing is ahead," he continued with hope in his voice.

Tanner and Luthy had walked with Knobowtee and Maritole for a while, but then they found a path they wanted to follow. When Maritole looked back, they were gone from sight.

"The women brought seeds in their pockets, didn't they Anna?" O-ga-na-ya prompted, "—pumpkin, squash, corn, beans."

"We have some seeds," she said. "There wasn't time to get much. The soldiers rushed us from our cabins."

"We knew this was coming. We should have been prepared."

"We didn't want to believe. But yes, I heard the animals speak. I saw the signs."

"Other cabins are nearly built," Maritole interrupted.

"Have you felt the place that calls the seeds into it?" Knobowtee asked Anna Sco-so-tah.

"I feel the seeds struggling to get into the ground," she said. "*Here*, I hear the spirits saying."

"Where?" O-ga-na-ya questioned. "This dense overbrush?"

"It's what I hear the birds say," Knobowtee said.

"I think the birds fool you," Maritole said.

"Think of the trees cleared. Yes, I hear the seeds in my pocket calling for the soil," Anna insisted.

"How can anyone farm this hilly, wooded country?" O-ga-na-ya asked. "Do you know the work it will take to clear the trees for the cabin?"

"We'll use the trees we clear to build the cabin," Knobowtee told him.

"Wait— straight through that opening— " Anna Sco-so-tah pointed. "There's another clearing. Just enough space for a few rows of corn."

"Each year we'll clear the trees for another row," Knobowtee said.

"I'll ask Reverend Bushyhead to bless it," Maritole said.

"I don't want his blessing."

"It's not his blessing, but God's blessing upon the soil," Maritole said.

She found a small rock and placed it in the grassy clearing to mark it.

"And where will you live, old woman?" O-ga-na-ya asked.

"I will stay at the orphanage," Anna Sco-so-tah said.

"Is this fair— that others have our land?" O-ga-na-ya asked in anger.

"What difference?" Knobowtee answered. "Does the deer ask, is this fair, when it is shot?"

There was a noise through the woods. Others were there.

"Yo— " Knobowtee called into the air.

"Yo— " came the answer from the distance. It was Tanner.

He had found a place in another small clearing through the trees.

"We were led here," Maritole said. "How else could we have come to the same place? Maybe our father brought us together," Maritole said to Tanner.

"We had a father," O-ga-na-ya said. "Maybe it was *his* spirit who brought us here."

Chapter Four

BAPTIST MISSIONARY MAGAZINE, VOL. 19, NO. 7 (JULY 1839), FROM EVAN JONES:

> *Our brothers are quite active in seizing opportunities to hold meetings in the various encampments and settlements; and very interesting and profitable seasons have been enjoyed by them on many occasions. I sincerely hope, if the Lord should spare our lives, we shall yet witness and enjoy much of the glorious effects of the power and grace of our blessed Redeemer.*
>
> *I have fixed a place of residence, about two miles south of br. Bushyhead's, which will be at a convenient distance for uniting our efforts in the work of translating, which is greatly needed. I have made arrangements to have some temporary cabins prepared, to shelter my family when they arrive.*

Chapter Five

Knobowtee and O-ga-na-ya began to plow the small clearing, but the soil was a shut door that would not open. The roots of the field grass were knotted in the ground. Nothing would tear them loose. Knobowtee tried to work into the land with a hand plow. Then he tried to chop it with a crude ax. He and O-ga-na-ya pulled at the tufts of grass. They continued to plow and chop and pull. O-ga-na-ya beat and beat the soil as if he was trying to kill it.

In the afternoon, Tanner came into their clearing. He was having the same problem. He had borrowed a horse to ride to the fort for another plow. He was going to ask for help in breaking the soil. Luthy, Mark and Ephum, Tanner's wife and two boys would stay with Maritole and Knobowtee while he was gone. Several of Tanner's pack dogs would stay also. They had walked the trail with the Cherokees carrying bundles on their backs. They stood by Luthy with determination in their eyes. The trail was still in the way they stood.

Maritole asked Tanner to bring Anna Sco-so-tah back with him from the orphanage at the church. Maritole needed Anna to help with Beulah and Rebekah, though she also had Aneh to help her. Maritole needed Anna Sco-so-tah when she pounded the meal and skinned a small animal. She needed Anna Sco-so-tah to build the fire. She needed Anna to think of what else they could eat. She needed a bucket. She needed a washtub. She needed baskets, and she needed and needed. Maritole also needed to hear Anna Sco-so-tah's voice.

Tanner's boys wanted to go, but Tanner left them behind. Knobowtee and O-ga-na-ya told the boys they needed them as they cut a few trees on the edge of their small clearing and carried them to the place where the women were scraping the ground for a floor. Knobowtee counted off steps for the cabin and placed the first logs in a large rectangle.

The next logs he placed for flooring.

"We can do that later," Maritole said. "I want a cabin."

"It's harder to lay the floor once the cabin is built," Knobowtee told her.

"I want shelter around me more than a floor under me."

Knobowtee and O-ga-na-ya cut a few more trees before dark and carried them to the place where the cabin would be, and let them fall, as yet without a plan for their placement. Tanner's boys carried small pieces of wood for the cook fire.

Somewhere it was written in government documents:

Whereas it being the anxious desire of the Government of the United States to secure to the Cherokee nation of Indians, as well those now living within the limits of the territory of Arkansas as those of their friends and brothers who reside in states east of the Mississippi, and who may wish to join their brothers in the West, a permanent home, and which shall, under the most solemn guarantee of the United States, be and remain theirs forever—a home that shall never, in all future time be embarrassed by having extended around it the lines or placed on it the jurisdiction of a territory or state, not be pressed upon by the extension in anyway of any of the limits of any existing territory or state; and whereas the present location of the Cherokees in Arkansas being unfavorable to their present repose, and tending as the past demonstrates, to their future degradation and misery and the Cherokees being anxious to avoid such consequences, etc. therefore, they cede everything confirmed to them in 1817.

Yet, more than twenty years later, just arrived in the new territory promised to them, the Cherokees were still crowded off their land. When they spread out from Fort Gibson to find a place to settle, both sides of the river, roads, and creeks were lined with cabins, houses, and farms, and fenced pastures were stocked with cattle.

Along the roads, the redbud, crab apple, and dogwood were in bloom.

Somewhere it was written in government documents:

Compensate for the inferior quality of the land in the new tract; for $6,000 to pay for recovering stock which may stray away "in quest of the pastures from which they may be driven;" $8,760 for spoliations committed by Osage and whites; $500 to George Guess (Sequoyah)— who himself was one of the signers— in consideration of the beneficial results to his tribe from the alphabet invented by him; $20,000 in ten annual payments for education; $1,000 for printing press and type to aid in the enlightenment of the people "in their own language," a personal indemnity for false imprisonment: and for the removal and establishment of Dwight mission.

The Cherokees would be given "a rifle, a blanket, a kettle, and five pounds of tobacco as just compensation. The cost of the emigration would be borne by the United States. Provisions for twelve months after their arrival at the agency and $50 provided they had emigrated from within the chartered limits of the State of Georgia."

Yet the Cherokees were hungry. The new land was farmed by others, or the land that had not been plowed was hard as the sky. The new emigrants had left their farms behind yet were unable to plow the new land. Tanner, Knobowtee, and his brother were from North Carolina, which had provided no compensation. Alone, left out, they faced the impossible task of resettlement.

Tanner returned from the fort with news that several men were coming with an ox and a sharp plow blade. He saw the logs that Knobowtee and O-ga-na-ya had left in a disheveled manner where they planned a cabin.

In addition to the seven million acres of land thus provided for and bounded the United States further guarantee to the Cherokee nation a perpetual outlet west and a free and unmolested use of all the country lying west of the western boundary of said seven million acres, as far west as the sovereignty of the United States and the right of soil extend— provided, however, that is the saline or salt plain on the great western prairie shall fall within said limits prescribed for said outlet the right to reserve to the United States to permit other tribes of red men to get salt on said plain in common with the Cherokees— and letters patent shall be issued by the United States as soon as practicable for the land hereby guaranteed.

What kind of words were those?
"Let them eat their papers," War Club said.
O-ga-na-ya agreed, feeling his fury rise.

Often, Reverend Bushyhead thought of the poverty of the people. The Cherokees had not received the compensation promised by the government. They had lost property and the possessions they had to leave behind. Often, he heard their stomachs growl during meetings. The old man, War Club, especially had a way of making noise.

There had not been payment for settlement in the new territory. The removal trail had cost them everything. Farmers demanded pay to pass through their land. They had charged to help bury the dead. The Cherokees had to pay for ferry crossings and forage. Bushyhead knew they had been charged more because they were helpless.

"We have to abide Bushyhead's prayer meeting," Knobowtee stated, as he prepared to walk with his family to church.

"I don't want to go," O-ga-na-ya said.

"He scours the Bible for meaning— for reason, when there is none. In the hardship of each day, I have to go to church on Sunday morning for a respite from this work. I have to hear Bushyhead fumble though this reasoning as to why this happened."

"It's easy to know why this happened. Greed. They wanted our land. What else is there to say?" O-ga-na-ya asked.

"He seeks some sort of justification— or rightness about it."

"I don't find any justice," O-ga-na-ya continued, "only expedience. Expansion. Just their right to take our land because of rules we don't understand."

"Their policies wouldn't make sense if we did understand," Knobowtee said. "Haven't we uprooted other tribes in our history? Haven't we moved others out of the way? I think it's been us on the move we should remember."

"What government is this?" O-ga-na-ya puzzled. "And our own people who have betrayed us?"

"Maritole won't let me out of church," Knobowtee explained. "You don't have a wife. You don't understand. I do things because of her I wouldn't do if she wasn't with me."

"Join us, Knobowtee. Why are you holding back?"

"There's a funeral today I want to attend," Knobowtee told his brother. "They've made a cemetery across the road from the church."

"They're also building a tavern across from the church," Anna Sco-so-tah said.

"Imagine making it all the way to the new territory, then dying. Why didn't they do it before the walk?" O-ga-na-ya sat on the ground.

Often, Reverend Bushyhead preached against anger. He preached against the secret meetings he knew some of the men held. He preached against conjuring. He knew the struggle between the conjurers and the Christians. Maritole felt O-ga-na-ya shift beside her the few times he came to church.

Bushyhead read from Zechariah 13:5–6. "I am no prophet, I am a farmer . . . And one shall ask, What are these wounds in your hands?" As he preached, he heard the hammering on the tavern across the road and men's voices above the hammering.

Knobowtee looked at his hands, blistered from plowing, as he walked back to the farm after church. He and O-ga-na-ya had stayed to dig more graves in the cemetery by the church.

"Don't listen to Bushyhead," O-ga-na-ya looked at Knobowtee.

"Be careful, O-ga-na-ya," Knobowtee told his brother. "I have listened to Reverend Bushyhead. There is something in what he says."

"You listen to your wife."

"Who does not know to listen to women?"

The new land was flat. The new land was hilly. There was a fort and a river. The trees were not as tall as they were in the old territory. They did not hold back the sky. Yet some of the same trees bloomed as they had in the old territory— the redbud, black cherry, poplar, dogwood, shagbark hickory, sweet gum, loblolly pine with hanging pinecones. Conjurers already used some of the bark for their magic.

"Did they walk with us?" Luthy asked. "These little flowers growing up out of the soil?"

"In the old territory, the beavers are stopping up the spring on Town Creek," O-ga-na-ya said.

The white settlers who came into the old territory were called Georgia Eminents. Would there be Indian Territory Eminents?—those who came into the new territory with the same authority to claim the land. There had been the Hopewell Treaty in 1785 to establish Cherokee lands. There had been the Treaty of Washington. The Treaty of_____. The Treaty of _____. On and on. Treaty. Treaty. Treaty. All of them— broken and gone.

Often Knobowtee woke with pain. He had blisters on his hands from the ax handle.

In the mornings, he found O-ga-na-ya already up, looking at the last of the stars. Sometimes Knobowtee knew O-ga-na-ya disappeared after dark and was just returning. He did not want to know where O-ga-na-ya had been. Knobowtee knew of the unrest. He knew of the liquor dealers.

Reverend Bushyhead decided he did not want the church near the tavern that had just been built. When he decided to move, the tavern owner and some of his customers helped Bushyhead and his men build another church. Knobowtee had not helped with the rebuilding of the church. He did not want to go anywhere but into the fields.

"We'll build your cabin next," Knobowtee told O-ga-na-ya.

"I won't have a place to settle until we've taken care of the three chiefs who signed away our land."

"You don't have strength for both revenge and plowing," Knobowtee told him.

Chapter Six

"The conjurers call for revenge," O-ga-na-ya said. "The spirits are unsettled until there is revenge on the traitors."

The groups of Cherokee men gathered in their old formations. The traditional Cherokees with their Kee-too-wah fire. The Christians in theirs. The renegades, of which O-ga-na-ya was a part, in theirs.

Knobowtee didn't answer his brother, though a question was not asked.

"You have a purpose, Knobowtee," O-ga-na-ya argued with his brother. "You nearly died with a bone in your throat when you were a boy. Remember?"

"Yes."

"Maybe you were spared for this."

"For what— the revenge you plan?"

"Yes."

"I lived to plant a field."

"A spirit pulled the bone out of your throat."

"Were you there?"

"Yes."

"I don't remember."

"You were too busy choking."

What did Knobowtee know of conjurer's magic or Christian faith? Both were pulling the tribe apart. He had conjuring in his family. He felt the presence, but he felt none of its power. If he did, he would use his magic to plow row crops on the poor, rocky soil. Rocks were his crops. Rocks. Stones. That's what Knobowtee grew. If he were a conjurer, he would return the Cherokees to the old territory. He would be on his farm in North Carolina. The ships that had come for several hundred years would be sailing somewhere else.

What were his ideas about revenge? The traitors should die. It was Cherokee law. But he didn't want to carry out the law. Was he a coward? No. He had other concerns. He had a field full of stones. He was having a meeting with the rocks.

Chapter Seven

"Are you asleep?" Knobowtee asked.

"No."

"I'm sorry for this."

"It's not your fault," Maritole told him.

"Whose fault is it?" Knobowtee asked.

"Momentum. The way a storm falling across a field is not the fault of you or me."

"Sometimes I don't think I can do it. The field-stones are piled by the field, and I plow up more. The conjurers say it is the land fighting back. Could you hold out your hand to me? I want to feel someone beside me."

"I'm not someone. I'm your wife."

A crazy world moved in Knobowtee's dream. He had taken a wrong stick. The others pointed their sticks toward their land and the land parted into plowed rows. Knobowtee felt he was digging in the hard, stony soil with his stick. Nothing parted for him. It was as if, once he got a small row plowed, it turned into unplowed land again. Dark clouds floated overhead. Maritole rode on one of them. He called to her, but she didn't hear. She had children around her. She was telling them a story. Meanwhile, below, the land turned dark as night and still she didn't hear his calls.

Maritole was telling one of the oldest stories. Knobowtee could hear a few of her words in his dream. The story was Nun'yunu'wi, the stone man, who was a cannibal. He could look like one of the Cherokees, but the people finally realized he was the one killing them. The medicine men drove stakes into him and pinned him to the ground. They piled logs on top of him and burned him. As he was dying, he told the people how to find medicine for their diseases. Then he sang songs the people needed for bear and deer hunting. After he disappeared in the fire, they found stones that they also used for healing.

Would Maritole tell that story to children? Yes. They had seen worse on the trail and in the new beginning in Indian Territory.

The monster who brought suffering also showed the way to relieve it. He left songs and sacred stones.

But it wasn't a cannibal bothering Knobowtee. It was his brother's anger.

Anna Sco-so-tah and Maritole prayed over the field, while Knobowtee and O-ga-na-ya plowed a new furrow. "Give yourself to them. Let yourself be cut," they said to the land. "You will carry our corn. You will become holy with corn."

Maritole watched the two brothers as they worked. She knew there was something between them. Sometimes the disagreement was so strong, they didn't speak.

It was the night meetings she feared. She knew the way O-ga-na-ya left the farm when it was dark. She knew Knobowtee was torn between going with him and staying on the farm to protect them. There were the Osage, Creek, and the white settlers to worry about. But that was not what concerned O-ga-na-ya. He was not going to let go of his feelings of resentment. At times, Maritole heard them arguing. Then they would grow quiet again. She could see the rift between them.

Maritole had been wrong. The march would never be over. It was a part of their heritage just as the corn, the deer, and now the Christian hymns.

The rumbling at night continued. Maritole stood by the window listening to them. Aneh was in the corner with Rebekah. Anna Soc-so-tah slept above them in the loft, because they couldn't get along without her yet. Knobowtee was outside with O-ga-na-ya and the other men. They had come back for Knobowtee. She wanted to drive them off with a stick. She thought of old chants she knew to bar their way. But she was a Christian now. She had to put magic away, or most of it. Instead, she prayed that God would protect Knobowtee.

One night, in particular, she woke with the stirring outside the cabin. There were horses. There was division.

It would be reported to government officials, that soon after their arrival in Indian Territory, Major Ridge, his son, John Ridge, and Elias Boudinot, his nephew, the leaders of the treaty party, had been killed by adherents of the national party immediately after the close of a general council.

Major Ridge was waylaid and shot close to the Arkansas line. His son was taken from his bed and cut to pieces with hatchets, while Boudinot was killed at his home in Park Hill June 22, 1839.

What fury inhabited O-ga-na-ya. What resolve drove him on a borrowed horse. What patience and quiet as they waited for Major Ridge. What relief of fury with the strokes of the hatchet. O-ga-na-ya was not himself. He was more himself than he had ever been. The frustration of the trail, the suffering, the moans of the people. His land being taken without his consent, but by theirs. Who were they to sign away his land? The arrogance. The autonomy. What was that word he was learning. What was its first act?

AGENT STOKES TO SECRETARY OF WAR, JUNE 24, 1839:

> *Boudinot was assisting in the building of a cabin. Three men called out to him and asked for medicine. He went off with them in the direction of Wooster's, the missionary, who kept medicine, about 300 yards from Boudinot's. When they got about half way two of the men seized Boudinot and the other stabbed him, after which the three cut him into pieces with their knives and tomahawks. This murder taking place within two miles of the residence of John Ross, his friends were apprehensive it might be charged to his connivance; and at this moment I am writing there are six hundred armed Cherokees around the dwelling of Ross, assembled for his protection. The murderers of the two Ridges and Boudinot are certainly of the late Cherokee emigrants, and, of course, adherents of Ross, but I can not yet believe that Ross has encouraged this outrage. He is a man of too much good sense to embroil his nation at this critical time; and besides, his character, since I have known him, which is not twenty-five years, has been pacific—Boudinot's wife is a white woman, a native of New Jersey, as I understand. He has six children.*

O-ga-na-ya ran to Knobowtee. His lungs felt like they would burst. He was crazed with the murders. They tossed him into frenzy. Why was he running? He was the murderer. He was the one others would run from. He was one of the perpetrators, not the victims.

He threw a stone at the cabin. He didn't want to face Maritole, who would be inquisitive. She did not know her place. She would act like she had a part in reprimanding him. Let her keep her nose out of it. Still Knobowtee did not come. In the dark outside the cabin, O-ga-na-ya made his owl call— a broken string of five hoots.

"What have you done, O-ga-na-ya?" Knobowtee asked in the dark.

"They are dead."

"Who?"

"The Ridges and Boudinot."

"Was it you, O-ga-na-ya? You wouldn't listen. You've brought this home to us. It will stain the farm. It will cause the chickens to hatch with two heads."

"You sound like an old woman."

"I told you not to be a part of them."

"It's over now."

"It will not be over. You have extended our hardships. Maybe for generations. Do you ever think of anyone but yourself?"

"I think of you, Knobowtee. I think of the family I might have. We have justice now. We can start over from the beginning."

"I don't want that kind of beginning. You bring blood to us. Go clean yourself in the river. Wash the blood from your hand."

"Someone had to do this. I knew you wouldn't. You would live as a coward. It is the Cherokee law you are always interested in. You should know that. Traitors face death. Treason is punishable with death— to cede away lands except by the act of the general council of the Nation. The Creek chief McIntosh lost his life— others— "

"I don't care, O-ga-na-ya. You've brought further turmoil to us."

"You have blood on your hands, Knobowtee. You killed a soldier on the trail. You have a scar on your face from his bayonet."

"I hit a drunk soldier away from me. I didn't plan his murder. Others jumped him."

"You made way for the others to kill him. It is the same," O-ga-na-ya said. "Archilla Smith, John Bell, and James Starr fled to Fort Gibson. It's guilt that drives them from their farms."

"It's fear of you, O-ga-na-ya, and others like you who can't hold their head."

"My only regret is that Boudinot's brother, Stand Watie, is still alive," O-ga-na-ya said. "He signed the treaty too. Now he's vowed vengeance against Ross. Some are urging him to flee. Maybe they'll kill one another."

"John Ross has refused to flee because of his innocence," Knobowtee said. "You set into motion what we will be dealing with for a long time."

War Club had ridden with them to the murders.

"What's that old man doing here?" O-ga-na-ya had asked.

"He's full of meanness," someone said in the dark.

When a shot was fired, War Club was in the way.

"He survived even that."

"The Raven Mocker who comes for us doesn't have anything to gain from War Club's death."

The men shivered at the thought of the Raven Mocker. It was a spirit, a group of spirits, actually, that robbed people of their lives. Sometimes the Raven Mocker flew through the air trailing sparks behind them. When they found someone dying, they made a call like a raven.

After the Raven Mocker kills someone, they eat the heart and receive for their own life the years that the person would have lived if they hadn't killed him.

Within three weeks, the national council passed decrees declaring that the men killed and their principal confederates had rendered themselves outlaws by their own conduct, extending amnesty on certain stringent conditions to their confederates and declaring the slayers guiltless of murder and restored to the confidence and favor of the community.

In August another council declared that the New Echota Treaty void and reasserted the title of the Cherokees to their old country. In another three weeks, another decree summoned the signers of the treaty to appear and answer for their conduct under penalty of outlawry.

The United States interfered by threatening to arrest Ross as accessory to the killing of the Ridges. In the meantime, the national party and the Old Settlers began coming together. A few of the latter who had sided with the Ridge faction and endeavored to perpetuate a division in the Nation were denounced in a council of Old Settlers. They acted in opposition to the Old Settlers.

"This is taking time from our farms," Maritole said. "We should be weeding. We should be preparing for winter. We don't know what it will be like here."

There was always news. Someone died of a snake-bite by the river. Someone was struck by lightning. Another fell dead at his plow handle.

"You walk two ways at once," O-ga-na-ya told Knobowtee. "You farm, you council. Which is it?"

"Both seem like plowing to me," Knobowtee said.

Sometimes O-ga-na-ya slept in the woods behind the cabin. Other times he was gone for several nights. Maritole smelled liquor on his clothes.

Was that O-ga-na-ya's religion? Revenge in the name of his god? Maritole heard fear in Knobowtee's voice.

"What if they seek revenge on those who took revenge?"

"You are innocent of this, Knobowtee."

"There was a soldier we killed on the trail."

"You were all out of your heads."

"We knew what we were doing."

"You walked shackled. Remember the feel of the leg irons on your ankles?"

Chapter Eight

Baptist Missionary Magazine, Vol. 19, No. 20 (December 2, 1839), from Evan Jones:

Before I left Arkansas, I made conditional arrangement to hire some cabins on this side of the Cherokee line, near to br. Bushyhead's until accommodations within the Territory could be prepared, and the prohibition of the government should be revoked; where I could in the meantime, pursue the work of the mission without much interruption.

I have just received a letter from br. Bushyhead, in which he says, the national council enquired of him whether I had made a permanent selection of a location, and intimated that it was their wish that I should settle near to the seat of government. If we should go on with the plan of translating and publishing books, that would, doubtless, be the most eligible location on various accounts.

The changes which the Cherokees have experienced have been attended with some evils. Several vicious habits have been introduced or extended, which will require the faithful efforts of Christians and the influences of the Divine Spirit to eradicate. We are encouraged, however, in the belief that, notwithstanding all the machinations of the grand enemy and his emissaries, the glorious work of our Divine Redeemer still goes on. Most of our members remain faithful to the Savior, and some have evidenced their faith in trying circumstances. And I do earnestly trust that the holy truths of the gospel have been so generally diffused among the people, and have gained so much authority over the consciences, that it will please Him, with whom is the residue of the Spirit, to send down his copious influences to bless and fructify his word, and grant a glorious ingathering of precious souls.

With regard to the location of the members of the churches, most of those who were not subject to the control of their friends, have kept in view the advantages of Christian privileges, and in their several settlements have provided temporary accommodations for religious meetings. Many, however have not made permanent settlement, being compelled, on their arrival, to locate near the government depots, and the places at which their detachments were disbanded.

Chapter Nine

Still, the men worked clearing land. The white settler with his ox and heavy plow traveled slowly to the small fields of the Cherokees. Meanwhile, Knobowtee and O-ga-na-ya plowed up soil for a garden. They cut logs. Maritole, Anna Sco-so-tah, and Aneh carried stones from the soil. Even Beulah and Rebekah helped. Anna Sco-so-tah made stick dolls for the girls. After the cabin, the men would make furniture— a table, chairs, bed. Eventually they would find an oil lamp. The women would make candles again.

Maritole also looked for a stone to use for a pestle, for pounding the corn.

Anna Sco-so-tah looked also. "Here is what the rocks say. The old fields will speak to the new. They will help us replow."

Tanner and Luthy, Maritole's brother and sister-in-law, and their boys, Mark and Ephum, cleared land to the south of the place where Knobowtee and O-ga-na-ya worked. Sometimes the families camped together for the night. The orphan girls, Beulah and Rebekah, slept quieter with other children. It was as if they knew they shared the beginning of a land they would continue to inhabit after the others were gone.

Maritole had seen the worried look on Luthy's face. She didn't want her boys getting sick. She didn't want them coughing like Beulah.

There had been rain, and it helped the man who came with the ox and heavy plow blade to turn over the soil. He even took time to let Beulah and Rebekah ride on the back of the ox.

They were covered with mud. Mud was every-where. It was as if the earth was eating them, was pulling them back into themselves, or into it. *Mud. Muddy. Mudded.* The object became the action, just like conjuring when Maritole heard the dark words that frightened her. The language that would build also would unravel, each working to destabilize the other, making resettlement harder, nearly impossible at times, because it set them working against each other.

"I want a cabin," Maritole demanded of Knobowtee one damp evening.

"It takes time," Knobowtee answered her. "Other-wise we'll have to do it all over again."

"I want a cabin now."

The next morning, Knobowtee and O-ga-na-ya lifted the logs for the cabin. Several days later, Knobowtee cut some bark for the roof.

There were those who came to the new territory in their carriages. Already their farms were built. Already their people were at work in the fields. Already there was pounding for sheds and barns. How did it happen that some men worked the fields with their hands, while others had men who worked for them? How did some get their work done, while others would take their lives? Some of the Cherokees had slaves. Some came with hired men.

No wonder O-ga-na-ya was angry enough to retaliate.

"I can't stand to see those men in church— the Vanns with all their property and land— Stand Watie, De-ga-ta-ga, *he stands*, standing at his seat in the front row— the Christian slaveholder and signer of the treaty that sent us from our land— singing out the hymns."

"Chief John Ross was there too," Knobowtee said. "Somehow they've gotten together again."

There were structural and economic divisions. The Cherokees who were poor had to work the fields they were given. They could not stand in their row in front of the church singing with strength because others were doing their work. Maybe Knobowtee's sons or grandsons would have the place he wanted. Maybe they would be the leader Knobowtee could be if anyone would listen to him.

Already things were changing. Many of the orators did not survive the removal trail. The Cherokees had to plant fields for their survival. They could not wait for an orator to come to the farm to plant the blessing. Or if the orators came, the field was not ready yet to plow. It had taken a long time to rid the soil of its stones. There were not clear markings of where the farms were. Things had been in place so long, they did not know how to start from the beginning. There were stories of orators getting lost trying to find their way to the new farms. There were stories of them disappearing on the journey.

"The orators blessed our field in the old territory," Reverend Bushyhead said in church. "In the new territory, we will have new ways. I will call a blessing on our fields from this pulpit. I ask God's blessing on each furrow. I plant this blessing for you to carry back to your fields."

Knobowtee had conjurers in his family background. They pulled at him. He could not always let them go, though he did not tell his wife. He listened as she prayed over the plot he and his brother had worked on plow for several days after the ox had torn the topsoil and broken the roots of field grass. Now it was the field-stones that stopped them every few feet. He heard old words of magic on O-ga-na-ya's breath as he worked.

Maritole was at the rock pile looking through the rocks to use for the chimney, the foundation of the corncrib, eventually a barn.

Knobowtee was careful as he built the fence around the field.

"I could have finished it sooner, but a quick fence would have fallen down sooner. It's worth it to take the time required for a substantial fence."

Maritole was angry. Knobowtee should be making shutters for the cabin and a door. She left the half-built cabin and walked into the woods. The orphans were sitting on a blanket. They didn't seem to mind that she left. Why didn't they protest? Maybe they had learned that nothing they could do mattered. Maybe they would rather be with Aneh. If Maritole's parents were alive she would return to them. Where could she go? She could live at the church with the orphans. Reverend Bushy-head would not mind. He and Mrs. Bushyhead needed help. She would live with the birds. She would live with the sky.

Maritole woke tired in the mornings. She felt she had walked all night. The people were still moving in their dreams. They had not arrived in the new territory yet. There was something within them that still struggled toward a home. But this place would be home. They didn't feel it yet as they worked through the day. In the night, their spirits struggled toward resettlement. Their spirits struggled toward home. When their dreams told them they had arrived, then they could sleep without dreaming of the march.

The girls suffered also. Sometimes Beulah's coughing kept Maritole awake. When the girls tossed, Maritole knew they must be dreaming of their parents. It was a loss harder than Maritole knew. She thought of the baby who had died on the trail. She thought of her mother. She thought of the children still in the orphanage. How many more could they take care of? She knew Reverend Bushyhead would ask them. She remembered a boy at the orphanage who looked at the girls as if he knew them, but the girls said he didn't.

Maritole gathered some twigs from the woodpile that the men had collected. She started a fire to cook some squirrel meat in creek water.

Maritole woke in the night. Something wet and sopping was beside her. It was Beulah in another fever. Maritole had grown used to her coughing. What had woken her? Someone else was there. She knew it. Who is it? Maritole could see no one in the dark. She looked at the door. It was closed. No one had been there. She looked back to Beulah, pale and glistening in the moonlight.

Maritole held her ear to the child's face, but there was no breath. She held Beulah in her arms. She knew she was dead. Maritole could not even weep. She did not wake Knobowtee. Let him sleep in his exhaustion. There would be time tomorrow morning to tell him. There would be time for him to see.

Maritole fell asleep with Beulah. The child was cold and blue in the morning light. She held her little stick doll. Knobowtee and O-ga-na-ya dug a grave a short ways into the woods. Maritole, Anna Sco-so-tah, Aneh, and Rebekah wept.

Maritole took the stone she had first used to mark their field and placed it on Beulah's grave.

Later, they would set stones in the ground for Maritole's parents, Knobowtee's mother, and their baby. Later they would set stones in the cemetery for all who had died on the trail.

"I knew someone was in the cabin last night," Maritole said at the grave. "Her mother came back for her. Beulah is with her mother now."

Chapter Ten

The Cherokees smelled of wood smoke and dirt. They were covered with mud. The dirt floors of their new cabins were caked with it, their steps into the cabins, their shoes, the edges of their trousers and dresses, their horses. Tanner's pack dogs were covered. But deer were talking in the woods. Corn would be growing in the field. The mud would dry. The Cherokees were listening for what they could not hear. They had memories with legs. Their memories still walked. Their walking remembered.

Their memories were the bear they pushed.

The impossibility of rebuilding was a bear— the enormous task of starting over. The mess. The weight of discouragement. Of realization of this next journey. All of it was a bear roaring with a deafening roar.

Maritole covered her ears in the cabin, while Knobowtee argued with his brother over the revenge that O-ga-na-ya had taken. It still separated them. As if they didn't have enough separation from the life and customs they had known. As if they didn't have this hard abutment to the void. To the nothingness. But out of the loss— out of the memory of communal fields— a word kept appearing— farm. Their farm. Individual. Not belonging to others.

"Yes, the Cherokees carry grudges," Knobowtee said to O-ga-na-ya. "Let them go. Let them go."

Sometimes there was a restless energy that made Knobowtee attack several different chores at once. Other times there was lethargy. The weight of his chores held him down, until Knobowtee felt he could hardly move. Whatever he did, his wife would find fault or tell him he should be doing something else. If only he could hear the bears talk. If only he could use their strength to plow. If only someone would tell him what to do and how to do it. No, he didn't want that. He knew what to do. Work and work. He knew he was responsible for his own doing— or undoing, if he didn't work— if he didn't keep going. That was his purpose. He couldn't expect anything to be finished, because it was not, and would not be while he lived.

Sometimes Knobowtee's chest jerked with a short breath as though a sob was buried there. He had to use his anger, his suffering, his grief. He had to be ongoing— lifting a log, plowing a field— one thing undone as another was done— no, not done, but begun. There was something tearing apart everything he tried to do. He grew angry because of his frustration. He gritted his teeth and plowed another row, going forward without getting anywhere. Sometimes he dreamed he was plowing in place. Sometimes he dreamed he had the whole earth to plow before he could stop.

Chapter Eleven

BAPTIST MISSIONARY MAGAZINE, VOL. 20, NO. 6 (JUNE 1840), FROM EVAN JONES:

> On the arrival of the Cherokees at their new homes, Mr. Jones devoted much time to visiting and collecting the scattered members of the churches. Some very interesting meetings were held, and several individuals were baptized. He had also selected a location for his residence, and begun preparations for erecting some temporary cabins, when an order from the War Department arrived, prohibiting, on certain groundless charges, his continuance in the Cherokee nation. The Cherokees have regarded this prohibition as a national wrong.

Chapter Twelve

Soon after arrival, Evan Jones was called back east by the missionary board.

On the removal trail, Evan Jones, the white minister who had led one of the detachments, loaded a wagon on an ice floe. He said it would carry the Cherokees across the Ohio River. But the wagon overturned and the people drowned. The missionary board did not recall him for that, but for another reason. When his first wife died, Jones married another woman, a hired assistant in his mission. She had an unmarried sister living with them. Her name was Miss Cynthia Cunningham. Somehow she was pregnant and died in childbirth, as did the child. She was found laid out on a board with the infant between her legs. They were buried together. Someone charged him with murder. Both mother and child.

Bushyhead would have to carry on on his own for a while. He wrote several letters to the missionary board in support of Evan Jones.

Eventually, Evan Jones was found innocent, and he would soon be on his way back to Indian Territory with his family.

Jones remained hopeful that he could continue his work of evangelism, though the Indians at first were suspicious. But when Bushyhead went with him on his circuit, they recognized Bushyhead as one of their own, and they listened to the gospel.

Some traveled twenty miles to the meetings. It was a way to confront the hollowness of the new territory. It was a foundation on which to build their lives. Some of them anyway.

With his helpers, Bushyhead built a house one mile north of the Baptist Mission. He called it Pleasant Hill. He built a ration station that was called Ga-du-hvga-du or Breadtown. It was there that government rations were dispersed. Some of the Cherokees still lived in clusters around the mission station, but most had started out on their own, though they still lived under canvas or in lean-tos made of twigs and leaves.

Bushyhead planted his farm and planted fruit trees. When Evan Jones returned to Indian Territory, Bushyhead gave Jones the house and built another for himself and his growing family.

Bushyhead dreamed of a school. He dreamed of a newspaper, *The Cherokee Messenger*, the first newspaper in Indian Territory. It would be like the *Phoenix*, which was published in New Echota— if only they had brought the letters from the type plate— but they had been scattered by the militia. Bushyhead also dreamed of shops, stables, barns, fields, orchards, more pastures.

He made lists, as he had for supplies they needed at the mission. He still carried the pages and pages of the list he had found in his pocket during the removal trail. He looked at it again— 15 reams Royal Demi Paper, 1 ream Retre Cartridge paper suitable for covers,

12 doz. Monroe pencils— there were over 150 items listed. He read on and on. Bushyhead folded the papers before he finished. How secure he had been. How far away those supplies, and that security, seemed.

Sometimes he remembered his farm near Cleveland, Tennessee. One morning he sat by himself at his desk and made a reclamation claim, as he had helped others write.

Wood and log house 23x20 $150
Log Kitchen 30x20 $100.00
Hewed log smoke house 13x13 $25.00
Log barn 60x22 $275.00
Cabin— outhouses $30.00
Corncrib 21x9 $20.00
2 acre lots at $10.00 each $20.00
122 apple trees at $2.00 each $244.00
120 peach trees at .50 each $60.00
Log cabin 16x16 $25.00
75 acres $600.00
4,000 rails enclosing woodland $40.00

He wanted to list his church, but Bushyhead felt it did not belong to him. It belonged to God. Bushyhead had converted to Christianity. He had been a minister since 1830. He had had a hewed-log meeting house, 35 x 25, with 73 members and a circuit of 240 miles. He had been assisted by Beaver Carrier, another Cherokee Baptist minister, and Evan Jones.

A sadness came over him, and he folded the paper. It was his preoccupation with objects that convicted him. He would not look back again.

Chapter Thirteen

"Plowing the land— the fields not broken— full of rocks— " Knobowtee muttered to himself as he worked with O-ga-na-ya and some of the other men.

"Nun'yunu'wi, the stone man, must have camped here," Anna Sco-so-tah said.

"Maybe there will be healing for us in the land," Maritole agreed.

The women and children gathered stones. The plow blade caught on rocks. O-ga-na-ya heard the clinks. Sometimes the rocks had to be dug out of the soil, because they were too large. The men sharpened the plow blade. They carried rocks too heavy for the women and children. They stacked them in a wall that bordered the field.

"I hear Bushyhead's baby cry at church," Maritole said.

"You will have another child," Anna Sco-so-tah said.

"Take a shovel. Dig out the rocks. Pile them in a row. That wall is too high. It might fall if someone climbed on it," Knobowtee ordered.

"The fields we are used to were worked for generations. They had been blessed."

"Our fathers, grandfathers, great-grandfathers plowed the soil for us," Maritole said. "Now we start over."

"The land tries to spit out the plow blade as horses try to spit out the bit in their mouths," O-ga-na-ya said.

"We finish our cabins," Knobowtee confirmed, more to himself than his brother.

"Wait until the moon comes out. Wait until the stars."

They sat together in the afternoon that was already getting hot. The women brought water in wooden buckets from the creek. Each family had been given one at the fort. After their short rest, the men continued plowing the field.

Then, late in the afternoon, the men called Maritole, Anna Sco-so-tah, and Aneh. They had managed makeshift rows that were ready for planting. The women dropped the seed corn into the plowed rows and covered it with dirt they pushed with their hands.

"We're not starting again," Knobowtee said, as if half-praying the seed into the ground. "We're continuing what our fathers and grandfathers did. It is just in a different place. I think they work beside us. We just can't see them. We set continuance in motion for our sons."

"You sound like Bushyhead," O-ga-na-ya said.

That evening as they went for water again:

"Look, Knobowtee, the sun going down through the trees. The creek reflecting it as though a line of light dropped to the ground. This place has a voice, doesn't it, Anna? Hear it?" Maritole said.

Chapter Fourteen

On Sunday morning during church, Reverend Bushyhead asked the congregation to take some of the orphans— if they had built cabins, if they had plowed fields— now they could take some of the children whose parents had died. Knobowtee had noticed a boy. He saw him again in the group of orphans in front of the church.

At the funeral, Knobowtee saw the boy again. He stood with a smaller boy.

"We could take both of them," Knobowtee said to Maritole.

The orphan boys were named Willard and Watson. They could have been brothers, but they didn't look alike. Maybe they had been in the same detachment on the removal trail and the older one felt responsible for the younger when they were alone. Maybe someday they would say.

The boys walked back to the cabin with Knobowtee, Maritole, Anna Sco-so-tah, and Aneh. Rebekah didn't want them. She held Aneh's hand or walked so close to

Maritole she kept tripping her. Maritole finally pushed her away, making an outward sign of the replacement Rebekah felt. She sulked and walked behind them for a while, until Aneh called Rebekah to her.

Chapter Fifteen

Reverend Bushyhead had ideas for the restructuring of the Cherokees in the new territory. He planned schools. He planned a temperance league. The whiskey dealers had followed the Cherokees to the new territory.

Willard, Watson, and Rebekah would go to school.

Often, they heard the sound of the horn that called them to meetings to hear more of Bushyhead's ideas.

War Club would be there on a stretcher. Would that old man never die?

The anger would not leave O-ga-na-ya, though the three chiefs who had signed away the land were dead. There were others still alive who had been for the treaty— who had more to do with it than he realized, O-ga-na-ya thought.

"How could I listen to Bushyhead?" Knobowtee asked. "All I think is awl, ox, hammer, farm tools, wooden peg, ratchet."

"I feel the common fields when we are in church," Maritole said. "The service is our fields that will never join again."

If only Maritole could see sparks coming from Reverend Bushyhead's mouth. If only she could see some of the conjurer's magic. If Bushyhead could speak like they did— if there was something tangible to hold other than hope and faith. If only there was reprieve from work and from the blind going forward they had to do to survive on their farms.

They sat on a stained blanket by the edge of the field to eat. Maritole, Knobowtee, O-ga-na-ya, Aneh, Rebekah, Anna Sco-so-tah, Willard, and Watson. Maritole had not had time to wash the blanket. She was afraid it would fall apart if she did. They were subdued as they ate, not as if sleepwalking, but sleep-eating. It was something they knew they had to do, but they weren't particularly interested in it. Once Maritole curled her finger around Knobowtee's thumb as she sat beside him. She couldn't trust her sight to know he was there. She had to feel his skin. She had to know there was bone under it. Maritole had trouble remembering. The others did also. From time to time, what they had been through seemed a puzzlement on their faces. The trail left them in a stupor of sorts— dulling its sharp points so they could rest from it a moment.

Chapter Sixteen

On a trip to Breadtown, Knobowtee saw a young man looking at Aneh.

Later he came to the cabin.

Knobowtee and O-ga-na-ya didn't know anything about him or his family. They went to their farm. It was disheveled.

"You can't marry him, Aneh. Think what your life would be."

Knobowtee kept her in the cabin. They never left her alone. If Knobowtee was plowing, Aneh and Maritole or Anna washed or worked in the garden.

Then, while Knobowtee was hunting, she was gone. How did that happen?

They couldn't take care of their own property.

"They haven't gone far," Maritole said, "not over a few minutes."

O-ga-na-ya left with his rifle.

"Don't shoot him," Maritole pleaded.

"I'm just going to scare him."

O-ga-na-ya soon returned with Aneh. She had run a short ways with the young man but had pulled back from him. They were arguing in the woods when O-ga-na-ya approached them. The young man saw O-ga-na-ya's rifle and left.

Chapter Seventeen

Long ago, before the removal trail, the Cherokees heard voices warning them of what would happen. The Nunnehi, the Immortals, who lived underwater, knew the people didn't want to walk the trail. They invited them to come and live with them under the mountains and waters. The people were afraid of the evil to come, so they had a council and decided to live with the Immortals. They were supposed to stand on a mound and wait for the Immortals to come. Soon, they felt the ground shake and heard thunder. Some of the people screamed. The Nunnehi who had already lifted the mounds were startled by the cry and let a part of it fall to the earth in a place called Setsi. The Immortals steadied themselves again and carried off the rest of the mound, with all the people on it, to the top of Tsudayelunyi, where it can still be seen. The people became immortal and invisible.

The people of another town on the Hiwassee River prayed and fasted, and at the end of seven days, the

PUSHING THE BEAR: AFTER THE TRAIL OF TEARS

Nunnehi took them away under the water. On certain days when the wind rippled the surface and the Cherokees dragged the river for fish, those who listened could hear them talking below.

Maritole and Anna Sco-so-tah talked about the Immortals they left in the east.

"Don't let Bushyhead hear you say that," Anna Sco-so-tah said. "He doesn't like for us to talk about the Nunnehi, or anything other than scripture."

"There was the story of an old man chopping wood, when suddenly the enemy came upon him— Shawano, Seneca, or some other tribe. He ran to his cabin to get his gun. When coming out, he saw a strange band of warriors driving back the enemy. The enemy was pushed back up the creek and finally retreated to the mountains. When the man went to thank them, the warriors were gone. Then the old man knew the Nunnehi had protected him."

"What is bad about that story? Why does Bushyhead object to our stories?" Maritole asked. "It reminds me of the Old Testament, when Elijah was surrounded by the enemy. He prayed that his servant would be able to see the invisible army that surrounded them to help."

"If only they could come now and clear land and plow fields and plant seed. If only they could chop logs and lift them on one another for our cabins."

"Usually they disappear instead of work for this world."

Once, a boy who was lost was taken to a settlement, where he was fed. When he left the settlement and looked back, it had disappeared.

That is the way the spirits work.

A goat came from somewhere with a bell on its neck.

"Drive it away," O-ga-na-ya said. "We'll be accused of stealing."

But the goat would not leave. Watson and Willard threw stones at it, but it kept returning.

"At one time, there was a Cherokee trader named Yahula with a little cart and bells on his horse." Anna told the story. "Then Yahula disappeared. No one knew what happened to him. But one night he walked into his cabin and sat at the table for supper. He said he had been lost, but the magic people found him. His family thought he would stay, but he got up, left the cabin, and no one ever saw him again. Afterward, people reported hearing Yahula's bells on the road at night."

"At Breadtown, I heard someone say they heard Yahula in the night."

"I don't hear him," Willard said.

"No, I don't either," agreed Watson.

Anna Sco-so-tah started calling the goat Yahula.

It wasn't long before another young man came to the cabin to visit Aneh.

Chapter Eighteen

BAPTIST MISSIONARY MAGAZINE, MISSION TO THE CHERO-
KEES, VOL. 21, NO. 6 (JUNE 1841):

Evan Jones, preacher, Mrs. Jones = 2
Jesse Bushyhead, John Wickliffe, Oganiah, Ooledastee, native
preachers = 4

*In the annual report for 1840, it is reported that Mr. Jones
had been prohibited by the United States War Department
from continuing in the Cherokee country, in consequence of
certain charges alleged against him. That prohibition, the
Board are happy to state, was revoked the 29th ult. by direction of the Secretary of War, on the authorized application
of the Treasurer of the Convention, "the Department having
become satisfied that the charges preferred at against Mr.
Jones were groundless, and it appearing to be the desire of
the Cherokees themselves that he should be permitted to
resume his labors in their country," a resolution to the effect
had been adopted by the Cherokee National Council, October 2, 1839, disclaiming all participation in the complaints of*

charge made against Mr. Jones, and stating that "it was the desire of the people and authorities of the nation that he should be again permitted to resume his labors among them."

Mr. Jones is expected to remove his family to the Indian territory early in the present season. During the past winter, he has visited Boston, and other places on the sea-board, with a view to promote the interests of the Cherokee mission; and by his unaffected piety and general deportment has confirmed the board in their previous judgment of his right to their entire confidence and affection.

The following brief history of the Cherokee mission, prepared by Mr. Jones on request, is subjoined, in the absence of a more detailed account of its operations during the past year.

After giving the location and boundaries of the ancient Cherokee country, now within the limits of North Carolina, Georgia, Alabama and Tennessee, and the history of the relations of the Cherokees to the United States until 1819, Mr. Jones proceeds as follows:

About 1819 the Baptist Board commenced a mission at Valley Town, in the northeast part of the nation. This region, situated in the mountains, was deemed the most enlightened part of the country. For many miles around, the gloom of heathenism and superstition had not been penetrated by the rays of the sun of righteousness.

During the first years of the mission, its efforts were chiefly directed to the instruction of the youth. Several hundreds were taught to read the word of God, and initiated into the elements of other useful knowledge. The mission, however, was not entirely destitute of spiritual fruit. At an early date three of the pupils and several white persons were hopefully converted; some of whom still continue to exemplify the happy influence of divine truth, and some have fallen asleep in Jesus.

In 1827 the plan of operations was somewhat modified, when the efforts of the mission were brought to bear more directly on the spiritual condition of the adult population. The divine blessing accompanied these labors, and several persons were soon brought under serious concern for their souls; and being directed to the Lamb of God, as the sinner's only hope, found peace in believing. Subsequent years have been crowded with similar results, and the cause of truth has been advancing at an increased ratio.

The introduction of the gospel among them greatly augmented the sum of human happiness. Where I was received evident and happy changes were produced, in regard to industry, economy and domestic arrangements. Houses, gardens, fields, personal costume, the instruction of children, the observance of the Sabbath day, attendance on the worship of God, and the abandonment of ancient vices and superstitions, united their testimony to the superior purity and efficacy of the principles supplied by the religion of Jesus.

Among the early converts was our br. John Wickliffe, a man of devoted and humble spirit. He soon commenced a course of profitable labor for the spiritual benefit of his people. In the spring of 1833, during a visit of the Hon. Herman Lincoln, the esteemed Treasurer of the Board, to the Valley Towns station, our br. Wickliffe was set apart to the ministry of the gospel, by the laying on of hands. He was proved a worthy helper in the labors of the mission.

In 1829, thirty-seven Cherokees and one white person were added to the mission church by baptism.

In June, 1831, the numbers were sixty-eight Indians and ten whites.

In June, 1832, the numbers were one hundred and thirty-seven Indians, eleven whites, and one black.

In 1833, a valuable and efficient addition was made to the mission, in our excellent and devoted br. Jesse Bushyhead.

Our sphere of labor was then extended below the mountains; and under the divine blessing many souls were hopefully converted.

Previously to April 7, 1835, there had been baptized, in connexion with the mission, two hundred and forty-four Indians, fifteen whites, and one black.

Twenty-three Indians had died, and nine had been excluded; making at that date, in communion with the church, two hundred and thirty-one Indians, fifteen whites, and one black.

From this date the labors of the mission have been variously interrupted by the agitations which arose in the country on account of an alleged treaty, ceding the whole country to the United States. Notwithstanding the obstacles thus thrown in the way, the brethren continued to travel through the country, during those troublous times, preaching the word in season and out of season; (until they were taken by the troops, to be sent off to the west;) and the Lord blessed their labors abundantly, to the awakening of sinners and the building up of believers in their most holy faith.

In the summer of 1838 the military forces, who had occupied the country since 1836, were increased to about ten thousand strong. Forts were erected by them in all parts of the nation, and at a time appointed the whole population were arrested and placed in forts, and within military lines; and were finally marched to the general depots, preparatory to being transported to the west. Some were then delivered to the United States agent, and sent off at once; but the great body of the people were, on petitioning the commanding general, permitted to remain till cooler weather, when the risk of health would be lessened.

During their captivity they suffered much from sickness, and great numbers died; especially among young children and old persons.

*Many thousands were brought together by these opera-
tions; and however painful the circumstances of their assem-
bling, opportunities were afforded for much evangelical labor;
which, I trust, was blessed to the spiritual advantage of
many souls. The brethren employed themselves in the
camps, visiting the sick, administering consolation to dying
saints, pointing awakened sinner to the Lamb of God, as
the only ground of hope; preaching daily in various parts of
the camp, conversing with serious inquirers, and instructing
them in the way of life. The Lord was pleased to crown
these efforts with the influences of his Holy Spirit, and many
came forward to testify their hope in Christ. Above one
hundred and seventy were baptized, on a profession of their
faith, and added to the church during their captivity.*

*An arrangement was finally made between the nation
and Maj. Gen. Winfield Scott, by which the conducting of
the emigration was placed in the hands of the National
Council.*

*On arriving at the place of destination, the first care
of the members of the church was to provide temporary
arrangements for the preaching of the gospel at all the principal settlements of the emigrants. The continued blessing of
heaven has attended the labors of the mission in the new
location. More than one hundred and thirty persons have
been added to the churches by baptism, and one new church
has been organized, since their arrival in the west. The present number of members in the mission churches is somewhat exceeding several hundred.*

*With respect to future operations among the Cherokees,
arrangements will be made as soon as practicable after Mr.
Jones's arrival in the Indian territory. The principal departments,
next to preaching the gospel, are teaching and translation.
Preaching is solicited in various neighborhoods by earnest and
personal application; and the effects of the long-continued*

unsettled state of society, antecedent and consequent to their removal, give additional force to these appeals.

In the department of education, two classes claim attention; children of families who speak the English language, and those of families who speak the Cherokee only, and who constitute the great body of the population. For these last, schools, can be taught by native teachers; but for the former, missionary teachers are needed. Much attention is required for the preparation and publication of books. Only a portion of Scriptures has yet been translated into Cherokee, and of this the supply has been entirely inadequate to the demand. One of the earliest objects of Mr. Jones will be to procure a new supply from the press at Shawanoe.

Chapter Nineteen

L ate one hot summer evening, the trees shook and the leaves blew down. The dust lifted from the edges of the field heavy with corn and battered the cabin. The clouds would blow in soon. The shutters rattled. The roof seemed to lift. Knobowtee prayed the roots would hold the new cornstalks up from the ground. Maybe the whole cabin would fly away to the old territory. The force of their dreams would push it back in the direction they had come. They would see their apple and peach orchards, their plowed fields, their running split-rail fences. But there had been soldiers on horses. The jolt of wagons. They did not have a chance to stay on their land in the old territory. Another bolt of wind shoved the cabin. The sky seemed to shake. But the moon was too heavy to move in the wind.

Chapter Twenty

In his field battered by the storm, Tanner looked for unbroken stalks. He dug fieldstones. He cut posts for his fence. He dug holes and pounded the posts into the ground until he fell beside a posthole, asleep for a moment before he pounded again, as if dreaming. Maybe it was his dream pounding. No, there was another post in the ground. Maybe the spirits came and helped.

"Rest between the digging," Luthy urged Tanner.

"I want to get this done. It reminds me of digging graves on the trail."

Luthy and the boys went to the creek for water until they dug a well. Usually they went at the same time every evening, so they could see one another. Mark and Ephum liked to see Willard and Watson. Rebekah usually held Aneh's hand and wouldn't talk to them.

For a while, Luthy was in her old cabin again. It happened often in her dreams.

"I dreamed of the garden of squash, beans, corn, pumpkin, peas. Stickball games, Green Corn dance, going to the water, even my parents were there— "

"When I work fencing these small fields, I feel like I'm building stockades for the corn," Tanner said.

"How long will we be on the removal trail?" Luthy asked. "How long before we know it is over?"

"I think sometimes I will see Thomas walking onto the edge of the field, following us from North Carolina. Maybe with a wife and child."

"You usually don't think of the impossible," Luthy said.

A few of the Cherokees returned to the old territory. Tanner had considered it but knew his family could not make the trip.

Tanner saw Luthy sewing, weeding, working in the cabin, until she fell into bed asleep.

"Let it go, Luthy. You can't rebuild in a day. It takes years to establish a farm. It will come— "

"The corn walked with us," she said. "I heard it on the trail."

"Is it possible to love the fields yet want to be away from them too?"

"I miss being with others on the trail," Luthy told him.

Near his field, Tanner killed a wild turkey. He shot pheasant, quail, and a deer that his pack dogs chased. He killed a wolf, but only because he didn't want it near the cabin. He saw the badger, beaver, bobcat.

"No, we aren't the first ones here."

At night when the dogs barked, Tanner felt Luthy shake with fear. He held his wife. He wished he could give her security. He knew she carried fear in her bones.

One day he returned from Breadtown with a child. A girl for Luthy. They named her Evelene.

"How old do you think she is?" he asked.

"Two, maybe three," Luthy answered. "She could be small for as old as she is."

"We will be ourselves when we eat our own corn again," Tanner said. "It comes through work— through plowing our fields— through not giving up. This is our prosperity in the new territory— the soil— the sky above us— the furrows straight as the trail we walked."

"Nearly straight. The plow still swerves around rocks."

"I'll get them next year and the year after and after," he told her.

The plow was the holy stick they followed.

The bear was their determination to continue.

Now it was the heat. As hot as the trail had been cold. It thawed the fears. It thawed their memories of the trail. The snow. Frozen creeks. Ice floes on the rivers. How many trails had they walked? In the night they woke sweating. Evelene and the boys were curled beside them. But at least, it was bringing the corn out of the ground with its shiny, green leaves.

Luthy's parents had died when she was a girl. Sometimes she still dreamed of them, then she woke with a start as though falling.

Luthy made a tobacco offering to the field, to the bare ground, as the men started to lift logs one on top of another for a small barn.

She made a tobacco offering to the mortar that would go between the logs.

She thought of her cat-lidded teapot bought from a trader. She thought of her turkey-bone necklace that had been lost somewhere on the removal trail. She heard the battle of the wind over them. The wind coming straight down through the trees as though to raise their cabin.

This was a different kind of suffering. Why did they think it would be over when they arrived in the new territory?

The orators had blessed the fields. Would the crows find their seed? Would they have to build a platform to scare them away?

Only the necessities. Only house, field, plow. Soon a cow. Pig. Chicken.

"What do I do with this injustice to chew?" Knobowtee asked as they met at the creek. "How can I plow and not think?"

Maritole talked to Luthy of her grandmother's quilts when they met at the creek for water. When would they sew again? Luthy probably already had her squares laid out on a worktable in their cabin.

When would Fort Gibson or Breadtown have needles and thread? Thimbles? Calico? When would they have material? There was nothing left of their clothes to use for quilt patches.

When would Reverend Bushyhead send off his list? Where had he sent it? Where would they get the money to pay for the order? Bed cords, dishes, knives, forks, soap, combs, candlesticks, scissors, all those things they had taken for granted.

Where were the deliveries of salt and sugar and coffee? The promised rations?

"I have something to say," Knobowtee said to Tanner, remembering an old accusation. "I didn't marry Maritole to get a farm. I wanted to farm. I just didn't know how yet. I am a farmer, but it wasn't as natural for me as it was for you, whose family had been farmers for a long time."

They had to have a day of rest. They had to have a day to not work. Otherwise they would not have strength to continue. Not everyone traveled to church. Some stayed on their farms, probably asleep in their plowed fields, or fields in the process of plowing.

In late summer, Tanner and Luthy worked detasseling the corn. Mark and Ephum helped. Evelene followed them with pollen stuck in her black hair. The insects buzzed around them as voices from the old world. It was as if the corn itself was buzzing as it grew.

On the farm, Maritole talked to the corn. She told it the old story of how it came from blood— from the blood of Selu when she was killed— how it came now from their words.

The words of their stories were like kernels of the corn. They had to be reminded. They were stubborn. Often they didn't listen.

Reverend Bushyhead's sermon was called *The War of the Winds.*

We didn't wander in the wilderness like Israel but made a straight trail from the old territory to new— well, we followed an arched trail that traveled north of impassable land with its dense woods and ridges. Not forty years, but four winter months. Now we are in the new territory. It is not Canaan. But what had Canaan been like? It was a place where the people worked to drive out the enemy. Don't we do the same here? We work each day to drive away our discouragement. We work each day to plow our unmanageable land.

They had once been hunters, who became farmers, who had been removed from their land. Now they were hunters again, poor, illiterate, lost. They were trying to become farmers again. Meanwhile, they hunted for food to eat. They hunted for meaning—for cause to continue struggling.

Would there be the large snake Uk'ten in the creek with its scales to help the Cherokees? Would there be medicine against the Raven Mocker? Sometimes, someone who wanted to die welcomed the Raven Mocker. But usually, they wanted medicine to ward off death. Would there be a medicine lake? No one had seen it yet. No, those were the old stories that didn't apply to the new land. Some things did. If they took up revenge, for instance, they turned into snakes. Other things didn't. They had departed, and the people didn't even know when they had left.

The words were places unto themselves. They would work sowing the little stones of words.

Chapter Twenty-one

BAPTIST MISSIONARY MAGAZINE (NOVEMBER 19, 1841):

> The Lord, in condescending mercy, is greatly blessing our feeble efforts. I believe our brethren are generally growing in grace, and in the knowledge of our Lord Jesus Christ. And the gracious work is extending. Since we arrived, June 25th, one hundred and ten Cherokees have been added by baptism. The brethren are exerting themselves in building places of worship. Our native assistants are faithful and zealous of their work.

Chapter Twenty-two

"A long time ago a man had a dog, which began to go down to the river and howl. The man scolded him, but the dog spoke, saying the water would rise and everybody would drown. The dog told him to make a raft, which the man did. Soon the rain came and the man took his family, with provisions. It rained for a long time, and the water rose until the mountains were covered and all the people drowned. Then the rain stopped and the water went down again. Now there was no one alive, but one day they heard a sound of dancing and shouting on the other side of the ridge. The man climbed to the top and looked; everything was still, but along the valley he saw a pile of bones of the people who had been drowned, and then he knew their ghosts had been dancing."

It was O-ga-na-ya's turn to tell a story. Maybe he hadn't told one in a while. Maybe he just wanted to tell a story. Maybe that particular story chose him to tell it. Maybe the evening moved him to speak. Aneh sat beside him as he talked. Rebekah was asleep with her head in Aneh's lap. Knobowtee and O-ga-na-ya kept their sister close to them.

They guarded her when they went to Breadtown for supplies. She sat between them when they went to church. The young man who now came to see Aneh sat somewhere behind them. He seemed to move closer each time they were in church. If only Bushyhead would tell one of their stories— but he stayed with the Bible.

"Awake, O sword, against my shepherd, and against the man who is my fellow, says the Lord of hosts; smite the shepherd, and the sheep shall be scattered; and I will turn my hand upon the little ones. And it shall come to pass that in all the land, says the Lord, two parts in it shall be cut off and die; but the third shall be left in it. And I will bring the third part through the fire, and will refine them as silver is refined, and will test them as gold is tested; they will call on my name, and I will hear them. I will say, It is my people; and they will say, the Lord is my God—Zechariah 13:7–9"

"What does that mean?" O-ga-na-ya asked.

"There's a cleansing going on, O-ga-na-ya. I feel it," Knobowtee answered. "We have to decide between the conjurers and the Christians."

"I believe the old ways," O-ga-na-ya said.

"And I believe the new," Knobowtee declared.

"It means something only if you believe it does," O-ga-na-ya retorted.

"Exactly," Knobowtee agreed.

"It means we have been through the fire. We should know better than to listen to the conjurers," Tanner said.

"We should know better than to listen to Bushyhead."

"But what if it is God speaking through Bushyhead? He says it is not his words, but the words of God. He reads from the book. Those are not his words."

"Don't get too concerned with religion," Knobowtee said. "We have our fields to plow. That is our direction."

Chapter Twenty-three

"You wanted your own life," Knobowtee said.

"Did I say it?" Maritole asked.

"No, but I knew what you were thinking."

"How?"

"By the way you acted."

"Maybe I have decided you are my life."

"Maybe I can trust what you say."

"I don't like it, but there is a God," Knobowtee said as he walked with Maritole, O-ga-na-ya, Aneh, Anna Sco-so-tah, and the children. "He doesn't explain himself. He just says that he is. He lets the removal trail happen. He doesn't seem to care that our farms were taken and we were driven to a new land. Does he know the work it takes to begin again? Does it matter? Is he enough? Is he all? Isn't he what matters? I can lose all. I can lose who I am, but HE IS. Isn't that what he said his name was? I am to swallow this lack of information— of explanation. He should pull us aside and say this is why it is. That should be his name. I should just get up from church. Walk out of the building. Not look back. That's what I should do. That's what God deserves after the march. We should act like he is not there. Isn't that what you do when someone hurts you? They don't matter. It's as if they never were. It's not because there is a hell to avoid. No, it is to be with Christ. To follow him no matter what. The removal trail is nothing. Suffering is nothing. No, suffering is something. It is the way to him— this God who sits on a branch and sings for us to come to him."

Our bed is green.
The beams of our house are cedar.
The rafters are fir.
Feed me with apples.
He stands behind the wall.
He looks from the window.
The winter is past.
The winter is past.
The voice of the turtle is heard in the land.

Now Bushyhead read from The Song of Solomon.

What if Maritole never had her husband's love? What if she always longed for it and felt its lack? This was the love she had. The love of the Lord. How could she understand it was sufficient?

"We have this life. We give it away. We receive it back," Maritole said.

"Is anything more difficult to believe than faith? It doesn't make sense," Anna Sco-so-tah said. "Nothing does in this place."

"It diminishes Knobowtee even more to believe. He has lost enough," Maritole finished.

Aneh and the young man who came to see her sat on a stump by the field.

"Why doesn't Aneh speak?" Maritole asked. She worried about her from time to time.

"She speaks sometimes," Anna Sco-so-tah said, looking through the window.

"It's the animals that don't speak. Maybe there were people not meant to speak," Knobowtee said at supper. "She is like the turtle and the rabbit."

Aneh smiled.

"That is not true," Maritole said. "We all have a voice. Silence is our bear to push against."

"Maybe you should be quiet as Aneh."

They put a stone marker in the garden for Maritole's mother and father, for Maritole's and Knobowtee's baby, for Knobowtee's mother, for Beulah, and all those who had died. They placed a stone in the garden for Thomas, somewhere in the North Carolina mountains with the eastern Cherokees. They remembered Mrs. Young Turkey. Kee-un-e-ca. The Widow Teehee. They scattered stones in a row beside the garden.

"The baby died. All that work for nothing."

"No, a life is created forever. The baby is with the Maker. You will see her again," Anna Sco-so-tah said. "I know he is with me."

"Who?"

"Kinchow— my friend in the old territory who died on the trail. I know it when I hear the chickens cluck."

"We have not been given hens yet."

"I hear them from the next world," Anna Sco-so-tah said.

"I know God was with us on the trail," Maritole said.

"I didn't see him," O-ga-na-ya said. "I would have asked for another blanket."

"Did you put a stone in the garden for Kinchow?" Maritole asked Anna Sco-so-tah.

"See it— that large, flat one."

"Are there two different truths? One for those who come into the land? One for those already here?"

"Who are you, O-ga-na-ya, after your rage is spent? What will fill that hollowness you feel? Protest kept you alive. Now what?"

The young man called openly to Aneh now. She slouched beside Maritole as they walked. Knobowtee ignored him as they walked on. Had they argued? Was Aneh like Maritole and carried grudges? Maybe Aneh didn't like him anymore.

Later in the evening, they heard the approach of someone.

"He is making noise in the leaves."

"He must be drunk."

"He doesn't drink," Aneh said.

Chapter Twenty-four

A neh was married in the church in the fall. He had a long name but called himself Edward. Some of the men wore turbans and tunics to the wedding. Some of the former ways had returned. Knobowtee and O-ga-na-ya built them a cabin in the woods behind theirs. Edward's relatives gave them three hogs. The men helped plow the fields. It wasn't long before Aneh began to have children. Rebekah was at their cabin more than she was at Maritole's.

Aneh sang to them but did not speak, as if she didn't know how, or as if there was nothing to say. But there was. The birds chattered over them in the garden. Sometimes she stopped to look up, to see what the unusualness was about. What caused them to make such noise when silence was the way to get one's work done?

Her husband did not say much either. Maritole and Knobowtee wondered what their cabin must be like when no one else was there to talk. Maybe they talked to each other more than anyone realized.

"Maybe they just didn't have anything to say."

"He looks like he's talking, but I don't know what he says."

"He says nothing."

"Maybe they hear one another."

"Maybe it's us that don't hear what they say."

"They have a silent language."

"No, the hammering for the cabin will be all the noise heard there."

"Maybe when we're gone, they talk until they fall asleep exhausted."

"No, they don't say anything."

"Maybe their voices are still on the long trip."

"Maybe they hear more than voices."

"What could there be other than talking? Nothing is there."

"Maybe their voices are ahead of them. They haven't caught up with them yet."

"Think of the deer. The rabbit. How little they say."

"Yes, I think of that."

"They have long distances between them."

"Yes, they do."

"Should we talk for them?"

"No. Let them handle their own lives."

Maritole thought of Aneh's life continuing without her. Aneh would do things on her own without Maritole's instruction. Maritole couldn't imagine.

"They are quiet as the sky."

"No, the sky thunders."

"The sky without clouds."

"The wind is part of the sky."

"It is part of the air."

"There's a difference?"

"To me."

"They are quiet as the well."

"Until you shout into it. Then there's sound."

"An echo."

"It is the same as sound."

"The voices talk to the stones that line the well. It's them, not the well itself."

"Or maybe it is the water."

"Yes, we have enough stones to line the well when we have time to dig."

"Yes."

"What do they say to one another?" Maritole and Knobowtee asked Rebekah when she returned from their cabin.

But Rebekah was young and did not know what to say. "They just talk," she told them.

Knobowtee stopped work one day in his field and rode the plow horse to the meeting house. He wanted to be present at the writing of the constitution. The Cherokee leaders were trying to find the words they needed. Reverend Bushyhead and the others listened to the farmers. They took notes. They asked questions. They shared their intentions. The farmers said what they thought should be in the constitution.

Tanner came to Knobowtee. He had plowed a field that a runoff crossed, and it was bogged in mud. It was too wet, and the crops would be hindered, if they came at all.

Tanner and Knobowtee sat at the table by the lantern, trying to draw a trough that would drain the field. That way Tanner would not have to plow a new field.

One day, as Knobowtee worked in the field, the horse kicked him in the jaw. He lay in the field. Maritole was taking wash to the line. She dropped it in the dust. Knobowtee was unconscious, knocked out by the blow. O-ga-na-ya leaned over him.

"He's still alive."

Maritole fell at his side. She saw the mark on his face. The blood. She saw the calluses on his hands. Willard and Watson cried.

"Knobowtee," Maritole called.

His jaw already was bluing from the bruise.

O-ga-na-ya was also over Knobowtee. "He's all right."

O-ga-na-ya lifted Knobowtee's eyelid. Maritole saw the white underneath. His eyes were lifted in his head. Maritole cried. Anna-Sco-so-tah was over him too, cackling as she did.

"Give him rest," O-ga-na-ya said.

"What happened?"

"He leaned down to pick up a stone and the horse kicked from a fly bite."

Knobowtee moaned. After a while, he roused and tried to stand but could not.

"Can you move your jaw?"

Knobowtee's eyes watered with pain. O-ga-na-ya tried to look in his mouth. A few bloody teeth had been knocked loose.

"We'll have to pull them for you."

"I think I swallowed a tooth." Knobowtee spit out another.

Knobowtee couldn't eat. He lost strength. Anna Sco-so-tah made mush for him. Knobowtee looked like he wore a swollen mask. Over half his face was painted blue.

He sat dejected on the cabin step.

"I have nothing for you, Maritole, but poverty, hopelessness, disillusionment, fatigue. I can't see beyond my labors," Knobowtee told her. "I don't know if our first poor crop will be enough to last the winter."

"I can abide your wounds," she answered, "but not your attitude. The emptiness you arrived with— "

"Defeat is more than I can handle," he said. "Why don't you go off with someone else?"

"I want to be with you."

"You left me on the trail."

"I am with you now."

"Will you stay with me?"

"Don't I walk beside you in the field? Grow corn for me so I can give it back to you."

Chapter Twenty-five

"Maritole!" Knobowtee called.

She turned to him angrily. "Don't call me like that. I heard you call from the road when the soldiers rode to our farm. Your words poke like a bayonet."

"Your words poke also," he said. "I called you because we've set up the arbors. I'll help you carry the baskets."

Maritole, Aneh, Luthy, Anna Sco-so-tah, the girls, and other women carried the baskets of *safkee* to the stomp dance beyond Breadtown. Some had come in wagons. Some rode horses. Most of them walked. The men had built the arbors of the seven clans around the stomp-dance grounds, and they all settled in their places.

The stomp dance was preceded by *a-ne-jo-di*, the stick-ball game. But during a lull in the play, the men bent, holding themselves up with heir hands on their knees. The crowd saw the thin bodies of the men without their shirts. The removal trail and resettlement had taken strength. There hadn't been time to recover. They were not what they had been before the trail, but they had to have the stomp dance. The life of the people was in the ceremony. It was an act of resilience— an act of alignment with old customs through which the old power came. It was how they would grow strong again. Already they felt release from the omens they had felt before the trail. Nothing fell the way it should not. The birds and animals sounded as they should. No baby had been born talking. The babies didn't say anything any- more. They just cried when they were born.

The seven clans were in their arbors around the dance—

Ah-ni-ga-to-ge-wi.
Ah-ni-gi-lo-(la)-hi.
Ah-ni-(k)-u-wi.
Ah-ni-twi-sk-wa.
Ah-ni-sa-ho-ni.
Ah-ni-wa-di.
Ahi'wah'ya.

The clans were the keepers of the earth, of medi- cines, of birds, of everything that was life to the Chero- kees. The people listened to the men's voices, the rhythm of the women's shell rattles as they circled the fire with stomping steps.

In the early days, four men were chosen by the Maker. They were called red, blue, black, yellow. They were given sticks to rub and twist until the sticks burned. Then the four sticks together lighted a fire in a pit, which was kept burning underground.

Knobowtee, Tanner, Edward, O-ga-na-ya, Mark, Ephum, Willard, and Watson danced. They heard the old rhythm of the land. They performed their ceremonies until they felt the magic that made things work. They had to unpack the old ceremonies after the removal trail. They had to find how to receremony the old ceremonies in a new place. Without a ceremony nothing worked.

The women followed the men on the stomp-dance grounds, moving their feet so that the rattling of the turtle shells tied to their legs picked up the way the women had always danced. In the shuffle stomp shuffle stomp, the ancestors and the old ways gathered in their dancing.

The old language became one with itself. It made a song— the way the sun reflected on the creek when they went for water of an evening made the water seem as if it were light. Yes, Maritole thought— language had light in it.

Chapter Twenty-six

BAPTIST MISSIONARY MAGAZINE, VOL. 22, NO. 2 (FEBRUARY 1842):

Department of Indian Missions, Mission to the Cherokees

[the following is in place]
Dwight—Jacob Hitchcock, Superintendent of Secular Affairs, and Mrs. Hitchcock; Roderic L. Dodge, Physician, and Mrs. Dodge; Henry K. Copeland, Farmer, and Mrs. Copeland; Ellen Stetson and Hannah Moore, Assistants and Teachers.

Fairfield—Elizur Butler, Missionary and Physician, and Mrs. Butler; Esther Smith, Teacher.

Park Hill—Samuel A. Worcester, Missionary, and Mrs. Worchester; Stephen Foreman, Native Preacher and Assistant Translator; Mary Avery, Teacher; Nancy Thompson, Assistant; John Candy, Native Printer.

Honey Creek—John Huss, Native Preacher.

Mount Zion—Daniel S. Butrick, Missionary, and Mrs. Butrick.

Chapter Twenty-seven

Now it was Tanner in trouble. A weakness came upon him. How would he care for his wife and children? How could corn grow from the land that had just been plowed? Some of the men were so discouraged that they could not work. They sat on the ground where they were supposed to plow. Sometimes the blacksmith or other men who were not farmers helped those who could not plow. Or when the men who know how to plow had plowed a few rows in their land, they went to help those who could not move. Some of the men could not get up. Or they refused to. They seemed frozen in place, as if the coldness of the trail would not leave them. Neither the conjurers nor the preachers could help.

Though Tanner had plowed some of his field, he too felt a heaviness on his shoulders. Often, he could not shrug it off. Luthy helped pull him from bed one morning with the boys and Evelene also. But by the afternoon, Tanner lay in bed again. He could not eat. He could not sleep. Often at night, he lay awake while Luthy slept beside him. He heard the stirring of Mark and Ephum as they turned in their sleep, getting used to their new bed. It was nothing more than a blanket over straw. Someday he would get cords and make a proper bed for them. Someday they each would have their separate beds.

Evelene could not sleep unless she was touching someone. Anna Sco-so-tah made her a stick doll that she had to have also. Often Luthy felt it poke her. The boys complained also. It was Tanner's goal to get the beds made.

One night Tanner fell into a fit of sleep. A horse wearing a red blanket looked at him. It seemed to be talking. Tanner had to listen. But the voice was silent. Tanner felt a recognition. Something was said. Tanner was helped by more than he knew. He had a knowledge of it. He was connected to the reins of the horse. They also were red, which was the color of war for the Cherokees. Yes, this field was Tanner's battle. He hardly knew where he was, waking sometimes in the morning, thinking he was on the farm in North Carolina. Thinking of the day ahead of him. The corn knowing how to be planted. The furrows knowing how to hold the seed. Then Tanner would realize with a snap he was not on his farm, but in the new territory. The new cabin was crude. There was not a long plank table, nor benches, nor cabinet with Luthy's dishes and teapot, nor churn, nor wooden buckets, nor iron pots and ladles, nor hearth fire, nor woodpile waiting outside. Tanner stopped thinking about what they had lost before the heaviness sat on his chest. Now he would get up. He had had a vision. He would walk the barren land behind his war horse wearing a small red blanket. The ancestors were there. Yes, they would walk the field with him.

Had the other men dreamed of horses wearing a red blanket? Or was it only Tanner? He would not ask them. Who knew what dreams were moving among the men to enable them to plow? On Sunday mornings, sometimes the women cried as they sat in church. The men also. But what was it that passed over them? A horse wearing a red blanket? A shield for the thoughts that would devour them?

Even when the pack dogs barked, Tanner could hear the old territory. There, he said it. Old territory. The former territory. It was gone from them. No, they had gone from it. It was not theirs anymore. It had separated from them— but it was with them, in their minds and memories, in their hearts and bodies. The land had been removed also from what it had been with the Cherokees. Others had come to make their own land upon it. The Cherokees were removed from what it had been. It was now another land. Tanner was on his own in a new territory with a horse in a red blanket he could not see.

Chapter Twenty-eight

War Club lay on a stretcher— the oldest man to survive the march. He wondered if living was his punishment. He wondered if he was one of the spirits already. He had heard them even though he slept in a cabin near the church. He was part of the orphans and old ones who had no place to go. No one wanted him except the spirits. That's why they hung around. They were always there. At night he lay covered with skins. He was one of the other world. He saw the Raven Mockers fall and rise again. He heard them chewing the hearts of the orphans they killed. It was easy for an unclaimed child to die. No one was there to protect them. The Raven Mockers could live forever on the hearts orphans.

What had War Club done? He was the heart of bitterness. No wonder they left him alone when he heard the children cry in fear. He could stand, drive them away with his hard heart. No Raven Mocker would eat War Club's heart. It would turn their stomach into rock. They must have posted a warning over him. *Do Not Eat the Heart of This One. Let him poison the earth with his sarcasm.*

War Club knew the war of the spirits. He heard them at night. He saw them fall from the sky to prowl the earth. They came as a hunting party each night. He remembered as a child hunting for deer with his father. It was what the traders wanted— deerskins. War Club knew the magic song to call the deer to them. He knew the sound of his father pulling back on the bow. He knew the sound of the arrow when it flew, and the sound when it struck the deer. He remembered his father preferred the arrow over the musket. Sometimes he thought he heard the deer sing their death song. He knew the deer had language. He remembered a hum in the air during the skinning, the dismembering. He remembered the deerskins piled up for the traders. The traders let the Cherokees keep the meat. All they wanted was the skins. He thought sometimes they would clear the woods of deer. Now the Raven Mockers came as hunters. How soon would War Club feel their arrow? Would it hurt? Would he see what was beyond this veil of life? He always had wondered what death was— or what it was like behind death. Beyond it. Would he hunt again with his father? War Club felt a stab of grief. Did the Raven Mockers also torture with memory? Then he would dis-remember. But it did not work. The journey he was on went back and back into memory. War Club held up his hand for his father to take it. Had he fallen? Had he stumbled once, and his father reached down to draw him up? How he missed his father. He had hardly thought about it but had pushed the memory far down into his heart. He had been nine when his father died. He was older than his father. Would he see a young man above him, pulling him by the hand? Would he know his father? What mirage was he seeing? How could he trust that he was still alive? How did anyone know they were alive? Was it all a magic show? Was it all imagination? Was it what he thought it was? How had he grown so bitter? He was prickly. Stale. He needed to move on. He called the Raven Mocker. He knew it was creeping around the corner of the church Bushyhead used for the orphanage. There was a young child there, sickly and too young to work. No one wanted the child on their farm. What good would it be? Nothing but obligation. Nothing but something to take care of that probably wouldn't live anyway. It was too hard to stay alive. There were too many things to do. They couldn't be pulled back by something that would not contribute to survival. They had to let the sick ones go, and those who would be detrimental to what they needed to do to live. War Club got up from his stretcher— he could hardly move. He was a narrow log or something that could not move on its own, yet he walked to the corner of the church where the orphans slept. He saw the Raven Mocker at the corner, ready to step through the window, still trailing with light, small sparks igniting as it tugged its weight through the window. War Club grabbed it by its leg and pulled it back. It made a high whine. War Club's heart was pounding. The Raven Mocker put its hand to War Club's throat. War Club burped. The Raven Mocker sliced War Club with its claws.

War Club felt a presence surround him. He reached for it. War Club, suddenly released from his body, rose into the air. He rose into darkness. Then a sour light hurled itself at his eyes, coming from the corner, square into his field of vision. He was in a land that was alive. He felt it breathe. It startled him, and he stood back from it, feeling it rise and fall like a chest. Where was he? What was he? He felt fear. Then he heard the corn talk. It sang the hymns he heard in church. War Club sang— his voice scared him, it was so clear. He knew then where he was. He was in the living space of heaven. In giving himself for the orphaned boy, had he accepted the Savior's light? What Bushyhead had preached seemed clear to him. He remembered the words that could be dismissed. Not believed, or even paid attention to. They had seemed inconsequential. A probability, at best, by the insistence of Bushyhead's sermons. They were hope when there was no hope. A resilience for their bitter helplessness. War Club had had nowhere else to go. He had stayed at the church for shelter and meager rations. War Club remembered how relentless Bushyhead's preaching was. Why hadn't he paid more attention? Then what was happening? Who were those people before him? They stood in the light that seemed to pass through them and hit War Club square in the head. They were a nation— they were— he recognized— what awareness swept over him?— he felt his legs fall from beneath him—

Chapter Twenty-nine

War Club's burial was held after Sunday services the next week. His throat was wrapped with a rag. A bobcat or mountain lion, Bushyhead wondered. Maybe a bear— no, it was a cat of some sort, though he knew people would say it was the Raven Mocker.

Afterward, Knobowtee and Maritole, Aneh and Edward, Rebekah, Willard, Watson, Tanner, Luthy, Mark, Ephum, Evelene, and Anna Sco-so-tah returned to their farms from church. They had only been gone a morning, yet the farm seemed a stranger to them when they returned. They had to start all over again each time they left. The silent morning. Tanner's dogs barking in the distance for all that had been. Maritole still mashed food for Knobowtee. Slowly, the soreness in his jaw was going away, and he was able to chew with the few teeth he had left.

Chapter Thirty

Maritole liked the early morning when it was still dark. She sat on the cabin step listening to the birds. She liked to sit by herself before she heard Anna Sco-so-tah stirring, before she heard the fire crackling in the hearth and Anna's ladle in the kettle. The birds chirped continuously. Their noise drummed away the silence of the night. Sometimes, back in the darkness, she heard a howl. Then she heard Tanner's dogs barking at the wolf or whatever animal it was. The voices of the birds jumped like insects she saw on the surface of the creek, hopping here and there, full of jumping whenever she knelt for water. Why were the birds singing? They were like the constant noise of the old territory pulling her back. She plowed her thoughts until they were like the birds singing in the dark, filling it with sound if not light. Did they ever get tired of chirping? Why didn't they just be quiet? Let them plow a field. Let them carry stones all day. See how much of them was left for singing. They were speaking to one another as if she wasn't there, as if her arrival in the new territory meant nothing. They continued calling to one another, leaving her out. One bird twittered. The other answered with sharp calls. Another interrupted with trills, leaving her farther and farther behind. Their chirps were as many as the stones in the soil. Maybe the birds loved their songs until they became stones that would not fly though the air, but fell to the earth and were buried in the soil to be plowed up by the people, the refugees, the forlorn ones who would come. Maybe the birds continued singing, scattering their song through the air like more stones.

"I heard Kinchow from the next world," Anna Sco-so-tah told them in the cabin as she poured mush into their bowls. "He told me to take Christ as my Savior. He said otherwise I'd be outside the gate."

"Kinchow was inside?" Maritole asked.

"He didn't say where he was."

Edward, Aneh, their infant, and their young child were there also. Edward had brought a slice of ham that they liked better than the squirrel meat they sometimes had.

"Come with us, O-ga-na-ya," Anna Sco-so-tah said to him as they prepared to go to church that Sunday morning.

"I think I should stay here. You never know who might come."

"What would anyone take from us? The air, the furrows, the boards of our roof?" Maritole asked.

"It's your guilt," Anna Sco-so-tah said to him.

"You took life," Knobowtee continued. "Therefore you wait to be taken."

With a sudden anger that startled everyone, O-ga-na-ya jumped at Knobowtee, nearly upsetting the table, pushing him hard enough to knock him to the floor.

Willard's chair fell sideways. Edward got his young child and infant out of the way. Maritole screamed at Knobowtee and O-ga-na-ya. Even Aneh made a noise.

When they arrived at church that morning, Maritole saw Quaty Lewis, whom she hadn't seen in a long time. Quaty must have been ill. There was such a change in her. Maritole hardly recognized her— she was old and bent. Maritole cried, seeing her struggle to climb the step into church. She had not left the removal trail, nor probably the memory of her white husband, who kept the cabin and field and let her go alone on the march to the new territory. She was still cloaked in it. The weight seemed to push her shoulders down, or the memory of the weight of it.

Chapter Thirty-one

Baptist Missionary Magazine, Vol. 22, No. 7 (July 1842):

> *We have great cause for thankfulness for the signal mercies of God towards us. We have been favored with an extraordinary share of health. The hot and sickly season last summer and fall passed without any sickness in our family. The winter has also passed without any symptoms of what is called the winter fever, which is often very fatal. The general health of the country has been better than it was ever known before; while the country left by the Cherokees has become a scene of sickness and death. The Lord continues to bless our feeble efforts for the advancement of his cause. Many are turning to the Lord, especially among the people from the mountains. One hundred and forty-five have been baptized since our arrival, and a considerable number more are expected soon.*
>
> *In regard to schools we are able now to speak more definitely. The National Council has made arrangements for applying the educations funds to the support of common schools. Eleven schools are to be established—two in each of*

the three larger districts, and one in each of the five smaller ones. If we had two teachers here, under the patronage of the Board, they would be appointed to two of the public schools and receive a salary sufficient for their support. One would be located about five miles west of this place, and the other at Delaware Town or Taquohee, among the members of the Valley Town church, and their neighbors.

With regard to the school at this place, taking all things into consideration, and particularly the fact, that the females in the nation are much behind the males in improvement, and that there is no school in the nation for the instruction of females much beyond the mere elementary parts of education, I think if a female teacher could be procured, competent to manage a school somewhat superior to a mere common school, she would at once have full and profitable employment; and I have no doubt, would very soon need an assistant. I have consulted br. Bushyhead, and other influential persons, on the subject, and all are agreed that this would be the most beneficial and the most efficient aid, in the way of education which, at an equal expense, we can render to the Cherokees. The school house they will provide without any expense to the Board, so that the teacher's salary and board and school books, only will remain to be provided for. The Cherokees are beginning to feel the propriety and the importance of doing as much as they can towards the education of their children. The intelligent portion of the community are now fully of this sentiment, and are disposed to act in accordance with it. The great body of the people however, are poor and not able to do much. I will write again about schools in the Cherokee language.

Chapter Thirty-two

Ephum had been sickly all winter. It worried Tanner and Luthy. She was pregnant again. Often she and Ephum sat together in the cabin. There was so much she had to do, but she didn't have the strength. Ephum coughed. He was pale and his skin was dark under his eyes. His seemed nearly transparent, as though he could step from the world without effort. Often he woke with nightmares, wet with sweat.

The conjurers came, because they had seen him. They said he had picked up a ghost while walking on the trail. Maybe they had passed a cemetery and Ephum had stepped near a grave. A Holy Man gathered the bark that healed from the new territory— the cherry, or acorn oak, or bitter apple, or a big white willow. Yes, there were willows by the streams.

The bark make Ephum cough. His fever would break, the conjurers said.

They looked at Evelene too.

Luthy woke hearing the scream of a bobcat. At least it wasn't a raven's call. She knew the animal called the fever from Ephum. Did his soul go with it? She jumped from the bed. His hair was soaked, but he was alive.

She knelt by the bed thanking God.

She felt anger too, anger at God that they lived on the edge of survival. Nothing clear. Nothing certain. But one foot over the edge, separated from death by a cough or a fall or a sudden weakness that came over them.

In the dark, she felt the child inside her move. This child who had been conceived in the new territory after the removal trail.

Chapter Thirty-three

O-ga-na-ya saw a girl he wanted for a wife, but he was harsh, demanding, and she fled.

What was hitting the cabin? Maritole wondered.

It was O-ga-na-ya, throwing small stones from beside the garden— the memory stones they had set for those who died on the removal trail.

"What are you doing?" Maritole ran from the cabin. She hit at O-ga-na-ya's arms as he reached for more of the stones. He shoved her away from him, and she fell on the ground. O-ga-na-ya went into the woods. Willard sat beside her. Knobowtee and Watson were hunting. She would not tell Knobowtee that O-ga-na-ya had pushed her. She asked Willard not to tell either. She didn't want to cause more strife between Knobowtee and O-ga-na-ya.

In the old territory, Aneh's husband's family had lived near the Oostanaula River at the confluence of the Coosawattee and the Conasauga rivers. He wanted to live near the creek.

"Is there any farmland that has not been taken?" O-ga-na-ya asked.

"Yes," Edward answered. "We found it near the double bend in the creek."

"It will flood," Knobowtee stated.

"We'll build the cabin on posts."

"What about the fields?" Knobowtee persisted.

"The silt grows corn."

"What're you thinking?"

"My family's always lived near water."

"You've been looking for other places while we built your cabin, plowed your furrows?" O-ga-na-ya asked, angry that he could have been doing other things.

"It could be your cabin when we leave," Edward said.

O-ga-na-ya looked at the cabin.

Knobowtee took O-ga-na-ya's shoulders, a gesture for patience.

"We fought the white settlers," Knobowtee reasoned with O-ga-na-ya. "The farms in our district burned during raids, the injustices, the removal trail, the murders— now you have to find what to do without something to fight against. Otherwise you're going to have to leave. Willard and Watson pick up on your turmoil. Rebekah is at Aneh's more than she is here. I feel your sharp edge— your strife."

"You're the white peace town and I am the red war town. How can two brothers be of different camps?"

"They're two parts of the same camp," Knobowtee said. "Dealing with failure is hard."

"You're a coward."

"I've found something else to fight."

"What else?" O-ga-na-ya asked.

"The farm. I'm interested in starting the farm. I want to take our defeat and grow corn from it."

"What will I do with my anger?"
"Swallow it like a tooth."
"It would leave my stomach empty."
"Walk the rows in the field day by day. Adapt."
"I can't."

O-ga-na-ya was away from the cabin for days. Knobowtee knew he was at the tavern. At times, Knobowtee wanted to be there also. He had heard the men laughing. What did he have to laugh about at the farm? But he dreamed of his mother one night, telling him not to follow O-ga-na-ya. Did O-ga-na-ya dream of her too? Was she telling him to stay away from the tavern? No, drinking was a dam that held back dreams.

Knobowtee was not able to help Edward and Aneh build their new cabin, though Edward had given Knobowtee two young pigs. But Edward had family, and others helped. O-ga-na-ya moved into the cabin they left.

That night Maritole dreamed of the stones hitting the cabin, only they were bones of the dead walking to the new territory, the stragglers, finally reaching it, knocking on the door to let her know they were there. Her father, mother, her baby. Look how she had grown.

Chapter Thirty-four

In July of 1842, Bushyhead reported a series of meetings held at the church lasting four days. Evan Jones had urged him to submit reports to the *Baptist Missionary Magazine* detailing his activities. Jones was always mailing reports at the post in Breadtown.

Bushyhead liked keeping notes and lists.

He could write to the missionary board that he had moved his church because of the noise from the tavern across the road. Some of the frequent visitors to the tavern helped Bushyhead and the men build a new church. When the tavern moved, Bushyhead wanted the church back in its first location. Once again, the tavern owner and his customers helped Bushyhead and his men rebuild the church in its original location. They made seats from sawmill slabs. They also built a shed for cooking.

Reverend Bushyhead kept notes of progress. He had signed the Acts of Union, adopted July 13, 1839, to settle differences and become "one body politic under the style and title of the Cherokee Nation." Bushyhead had helped write the Cherokee constitution. He had been elected chief justice of the Cherokee Nation in 1840.

In 1841, Bushyhead was also president of the Cherokee Bible Society, which he organized.

He founded the Female Seminary in 1842. It was a brick building that served as a meetinghouse for services and a schoolhouse for conducting classes. The building opened December 1, 1843.

Also in 1843, the Baptist Mission Board in Boston furnished a press and type for the Baptist Mission at Cherokee. Jesse Bushyhead and Evan Jones worked at translating the Scriptures into Cherokee. They were finally able to print portions of the Book.

Bushyhead became the first president of the Going-Snake Temperance Society, organized in 1844. Alcohol had been a problem even before they left the old territory. The whiskey traffic followed them to the new territory. He had had trouble in his early life with it. He knew its dangers. He knew some of his congregation stopped at the tavern.

The first issue of Oklahoma's first newspaper, *The Cherokee Messenger*, was printed August 1844. The first issue contained an account of the meeting of the Going-Snake Temperance Society.

Bushyhead remained suspect to Knobowtee and O-ga-na-ya. He was friends with John Ross and Stand Watie, whom they did not like. Bushyhead was the leader of the Ross faction but at the same time connected with the Ridge faction. He settled difficulties on both sides: Old Settlers and new immigrants.

"He's a Christian," Maritole told Knobowtee. "He has help that you don't. Remember that when you stay home from church."

Reverend Bushyhead felt his work was a lasso he threw into the future, hoping it would catch on something and secure the Cherokees. Then they could pull themselves ahead as a nation.

Chapter Thirty-five

A nna Sco-so-tah called like a hen.

"She's returned to herself," Knobowtee looked up from the field.

There was a large cloud coming over the trees.

"Another storm," Maritole said.

"This place is wild with them. One tromps through after another. I think the spirits are behind them. I think they do anything to cause us trouble."

There was a flash of lightning. The low rumble of thunder followed. They could feel the rumble with their feet. Another flash of lightning seemed to strike close to their cabin.

Anna Sco-so-tah rushed from the cabin, squawking. Maritole and Knobowtee went to see what was wrong. They ran through the field as the hard, cold drops began to fall.

"I knew it was coming," Anna Sco-so-tah said. "I felt the strike before it hit."

"Hit what?"

"That old pot. The lightning hit the cooking pot instead of the cabin."

They looked at the small crater.

"Don't touch it," Knobowtee warned.

Maritole had buried the cooking pot beside the cabin, just under the soil. It was the cooking pot Maritole brought from the old territory. It had been dented, crusted. She could not use it any longer. She had kept it because she remembered her mother's hand on it.

"I think my parents have arrived in the new territory," Maritole said. "I think they went on to the afterworld with their first granddaughter."

"Mrs. Young Turkey walked into the ghost world. She went on one of her stories. I can see her in the land of the ghosts," Anna Sco-so-tah said. "Sometimes I see them— Kee-un-e-ca, Mrs. Young Turkey, the Widow Teehee— "

Knobowtee pulled the two women into the cabin and closed the door against the clumps of rain.

Chapter Thirty-six

BAPTIST MISSIONARY MAGAZINE, VOL. 22, NO. 9 (SEPTEMBER 1842):

It is with pleasure I give you some further account of the progress of the word of grace among the Cherokees. I cannot but feel greatly encouraged in the hope that the conquests of our blessed Redeemer will be repeated and extended in this country, although there are still formidable obstacles—many strong holds of sin to be subdued.

July 4 We concluded a series of meetings of four days continuance with the Amohee church. At the monthly meeting in June, the brethren determined to continue the next monthly meeting for four days, and also to erect a shed at a more convenient place. They met accordingly and erected a substantial shed, seventy feet by thirty, and filled it with convenient seats, of saw-mill slabs. They also made a smaller shed for cooking, and provided comfortable refreshments for those who chose to remain on the ground during the meeting. Two years ago, the church used to meet at this place, before under a temporary shed, but a whiskey shop being set up within a few yards, which greatly annoyed them, they built a small meeting-house about two miles off. The house having become entirely too small, they fixed on the old place again, and now, to the praise of gospel influence, the man who once annoyed them with his whiskey shop, assisted with labor and provisions to build the shed, and fitted up the same cabin, and furnished provisions for the comfortable accommodations of the preacher and others coming from a distance to attend meetings.

Religious exercise commenced on Friday the 1st inst. but on account of heavy rains few attended. On Saturday, there was a very large congregation, and serious attention. Several persons cheered our hearts by the profession of "repentance toward God and faith in our Lord Jesus Christ." Many of the brethren and inquirers devoted great part of the night to the exercises of prayer and praise. Meeting for prayer and expounding a portion of scripture, was held at sunrise Sabbath morning. After breakfast, the church assembled to hear the relations of candidates for baptism. A colored woman, a member of our late brother O'Bryant's church, was received, on evidence of Christian character. At eleven, preaching commenced. The place was completely crowded, and many outside. Solemn attention pervaded the assembly, and some appeared much affected. After preaching the whole congregation proceeded through a grove, along a grassy walk, two hundred and fifty yards, to a beautiful stream, in which I had the pleasure to baptize twelve Cherokees, six males and six females, and one black, on a hopeful profession of faith in the Savior of sinners. After a short interval, a large company of Cherokees sat down to commemorate the death of our adorable Redeemer. At night, brethren Foster and Oganiah preached, and invited the anxious to unite with the church in prayer. About thirty came forward; so we hope the work is still going on. The exercises were continued till Monday noon, when we parted, greatly refreshed in spirit, and encouraged to expect the further triumphs of the Savior's cause.

July 9 & 10—at Taquohee. Two days' meeting. A very large congregation. The house, 40 feet by 20, crowded, and many more outside than in the house. Received and baptized five Cherokee males three females. Administered the sacrament of the Lord's supper to a large and deeply devout assembly; all Cherokees. At night a number of anxious inquirers came forward for prayer.

July 16 & 17—Two days' meeting at Tseyohee. A large, attentive congregation. Three males and one female baptized: all Cherokees.

Chapter Thirty-seven

Luthy had a girl, Annohee. She now had four children. Rebekah was with Aneh, because she liked to be around her babies. Sometimes Willard and Watson stayed with Mark and Ephum. Maritole would have no one. She prayed in church, singing sometimes at meetings after Knobowtee left with Tanner and Luthy, who were too busy to stay at the church. When she saw Annohee baptized, Maritole wanted to be baptized. She wanted Rebekah, Willard, and Watson baptized. She wanted to be married at the church.

Then Maritole realized she was pregnant.

She told Knobowtee. She told Anna Sco-so-tah. She told Luthy, grabbing up Annohee as she entered their cabin. Feeling the tears on her face, she wet her finger with her tears and marked Annohee's forehead with a cross and sang an old song to help one going on a road:

> nv:no:hi   vdovi   ahl(i)sde:hl(v)doꞏdi
> road   going   to help one

Chapter Thirty-eight

Anna Sco-so-tah prayed in the field as the sun came up.

"What are you praising?" O-ga-na-ya asked. "The mud?"

"There is a preacher by your name. Oganiah," Anna Sco-so-tah said.

"Close to it," O-ga-na-ya said. "What do you mean by it?"

"Nothing. I just thought you should know."

"I won't go to the church," O-ga-na-ya told her. "I would see Stand Watie, slave owner and traitor. He should have been killed like his brother, Elias Boudinot, like his uncle, Major Ridge, and his cousin, John Ridge. Now Stand Watie's the clerk of the Cherokee Supreme Court."

"Church would wash the blood from your hands."

"A justified blood doesn't stain."

"There is no justification in men spilling blood."

O-ga-na-ya thought about what the old woman had said. She was mainly an annoyance, but her words stayed with him.

Chapter Thirty-nine

How the names of the old territory struck a pain in Bushyhead when they crossed his mind. He wrote them in the margins of his translation work. He wrote the words he heard from his congregation— place-names— memories of where they had come from— where they had been when such and such happened in the old territory— Coosawatee. Long Swamp. Stills. Amagalolega. Big Savannah. Deganeetla. Tinsawattee.

How the memories jolted him. Whether translating the Bible, or laying fence, or preaching the words of the Bible, he felt the precision it took. The Cherokees had been the carriers of corn to the new territory. In their memories, they also carried fork, plate, china bowl, crock, bucket, ladle, quilts worn from the sharp edges of the trail. They also carried words. Bushyhead felt the old language buck under the yoke of translation. Sometimes the old words did not want carry the new message of Christianity. But despite the tedious work of stretching and bending the old language— despite the rain, hardship, and uncertainty of everything, Bushyhead had a cabin for his family and a log

church with hewn seats and a pulpit. He had fragments of notes and conversations that went through
his head.

Often Bushyhead sat in a chair at a small table at Evan
Jones's house. They had the puzzling work of translating
the English Bible into Cherokee. Working with two different languages that didn't mix was like working in a
field with two different crops coming up. Only they were
so different, they couldn't both be called crops.

Sometimes Evan Jones would translate English
words into Cherokee, but they didn't carry the Cherokee language. The ground was stumps where there
should have been trees.

God had confounded language. When one group of
people spoke, it sounded like babble to another group.
But Bushyhead had to work to place a splint on the
old break of language. How hard it was to put the language back together. The Cherokees had to be able to
read the Bible in their own language. They had to be
standing in the woods they knew. Either that, or teach
the Cherokees English. And when could Bushyhead
do that? Was it possible to call them in from their
fields to learn a new language? Was it possible for him
to take on one more task?

Language was like the story of the bear that came
alive after it was dead, skinned, divided, and its parts
distributed to the people. Yet it lived as a bear again.

Language was a bird whose wings opened and
changed when it flew.

A bird was sitting on a branch outside the front
door of Jones's house. Its voice entered the room, where
the walls held it, echoing there, seeming louder inside
than out, where it spread upon the air.

Bushyhead struggled to understand his thoughts. They came mixed and confused. It was the same as if one bird changed into another. The same was in the beginning with God. To break the necessary brokenness of our tongues. The Lord scattered one language into many in Genesis 11:8. He confounded language for a purpose— so the people wouldn't become strong in themselves— so they wouldn't be united in building something they should not build. Now Bushyhead worked to bring the Lord's words to the people in their own way.

In his discouragement, he sometimes thought language was a Raven Mocker. It was more than one but had a singular name. Translation ate the heart of another. It stole the essence of one language and changed it into another.

Language was a conjurer.

Bushyhead also visited the Cherokees who still remained at Fort Gibson. They could not be persuaded to go into the woods and find a clearing to start again. They were so devoid of will that they sat like the bushes. Some of them were so sick, Bushyhead had to build another place by the church to house the sick of mind, of soul, of will.

How many drank and hit their wives and children? How many gave up and killed themselves or starved? How many could not get around the depression and discouragement that still camped before them?

"Did the murders settle your urge for revenge?" Reverend Bushyhead asked O-ga-na-ya when he found him on the road. "Didn't it stir up more contention, especially in you?"

O-ga-na-ya tried to focus. Bushyhead could see O-ga-na-ya struggling to recognize him. Bushyhead dismounted from his horse. "I know what it feels like to drink," Bushyhead told him. He could almost read O-ga-na-ya's thoughts. "Yes, it's who you think it is," Bushyhead told him. "Before I became a minister, I numbed myself with the trader's whiskey. I've prayed for you when I saw you stumble from the door of the tavern."

Chapter Forty

Maritole held Luthy's baby, Annohee, who looked beyond her shoulder as if she was seeing others above her. To the Cherokees, there was no separation between past and present. There and here. This world was not bound to itself, but could cross over into the other. Annohee was looking at the other world that had sent her to Luthy and not Maritole. Anohee was looking while she could still see the spirit world, before it became invisible to her. Was it Maritole's baby there in the other world looking at Annohee, who would be her cousin? How a baby lived in a world inside them and above them. How the worlds were joined in a baby. How the one was connected to the other. Maritole watched as Annohee's eyes followed someone above her whom Maritole could not see. She thought again it might be the soul of the baby she carried. Maritole knew she was not bound to this world either. The conjurers' magic was a pathway. The conjurers could touch that world. They were a conduit for it. The spirit world crossed in them. If Maritole thought of the conjurers long enough, she could feel the pathway too. She could cross and see her baby who died, her mother—

"Maritole," Luthy called her back. "Here, let me take the baby."

After Luthy's milk, a small cluster of cornmeal was mixed with Luthy's milk for Annohee. It kicked and fretted.

Mark and Ephum worked in the field with Tanner. Willard and Watson followed. Maritole could hear Tanner's voice as he called to the boys this way or that. Evelene and Rebekah played near the cabin. Anna Sco-so-tah was washing kettles. Luthy and even Aneh had Anna Sco-So-tah now to help them, because they needed her help more than Maritole did. Let the whole world come and live with Luthy and Aneh and leave Maritole alone.

Why was she alone when she had been surrounded by everyone? Maritole wondered what had happened to her relatives from Red Clay, Tennessee. The Cherokees were now spread over the new territory. There was no way for them to know where the others were. Maybe she would read about them in *The Cherokee Messenger*, except that she could not read. Maybe she would see them at Breadtown or at the church meetings. Sometimes at church, she recognized others who had been in their detachment on the removal trail. Would she know the rest if she saw them? Had the hardness of the trail changed them so she did not recognize them? Would they recognize her? What did she look like?

If only she knew how to write. But then she would have to know how to read also. She wanted her child to read. It would go to school.

Maritole listened as Anna Sco-so-tah read the new Bible. Knobowtee listened also, when he came in from the field at night.

"How do you know how to read?"

"Maybe I'm making it up."

"No one could make up something like that."

Chapter Forty-one

Knobowtee found O-ga-na-ya waking from a stupor one morning, when he went to his cabin.

"What are you doing, O-ga-na-ya?" Knobowtee asked. "Will this become habit?"

Knobowtee let him sleep the rest of the morning then returned with food, but O-ga-na-ya didn't want to eat.

"We're drowning as if water flowed over us," O-ga-na-ya said. "Bushyhead would say we're Noah without an ark."

"No, our ark is work," Knobowtee told him. "It's keeping us afloat."

"That's your opinion," O-ga-na-ya said.

"We'll float on these difficulties by our efforts— our slow accomplishments— we have our crude cabins, our half-plowed fields."

"A few accomplishments, but most of our steps are backward."

O-ga-na-ya was right. The corn was patchy. There were bare spots on the ground. The stalks were uneven heights. There were not many kernels on the cobs. The corn was not growing together but remained separate stalks. They had to learn to grow together. The stalks had to learn to speak to the soil.

All this for a few stalks of corn—

No, O-ga-na-ya was wrong, Knobowtee thought as he watched Maritole, his pregnant wife, with pleasure. The corn was speaking to the ground. It was telling the stones to move over. It was telling the ground it had come to the new territory. Get used to it. This soil had been lazy. Now it had to learn to accommodate the corn.

Where was her father's stand-up song for the corn?— Maritole tried to remember. How had he sung it? Why hadn't she learned it? Why hadn't she known she would be responsible for carrying the old messages they needed? No one had told her. Had she paid attention to anything?— she asked herself. How could everything certain go away?

Maritole lifted her nose in a sudden breeze. Luthy was cooking with something new she had picked, probably along the creek when she went for water. Luthy always was finding different plants to mix with the squirrel or deer meat. Knobowtee probably was thinking he would like Maritole to find something new. No, it was corn he wanted.

Would the Cherokees ever need to build corncribs again?

That night Maritole turned with a cramp. She heard stirring from Anna Sco-so-tah's corner of the cabin. Maritole knew her feet were walking in her sleep.

Go back to the old territory, Maritole thought. Find the words we left there— or just stay here and dream where the plants are. Maritole fell back into sleep remembering the taste of peaches and berries.

Chapter Forty-two

Reverend Jesse Bushyhead liked the book of Nehemiah. It reminded him of the Cherokee festivals. It reminded him of their revivals and brush-arbor meetings.

The book of Nehemiah was about rebuilding. How Bushyhead needed the Scripture for instruction. How they worked at translation.

History was important to God. Look in the ninth chapter, how the march of the Hebrews through the wilderness was recorded. Thou, even thou, are Lord alone; you made heaven, the heaven of heavens, with all their host, the earth, and all things that are therein, the seas, and all that is therein, and you preserved them all, and the host of heaven worshipped you.

God had chosen Abraham, he called Moses and divided the sea to remove the Hebrews from Egypt. Did God not also remove the Cherokees, though their cry had been to stay on their land? God led the Hebrews with a pillar of fire and with a cloud. He gave the laws. He gave them water from a rock. Had that happened on the trail? No, they hadn't needed water. They could eat the snow. Had they had manna? Had quail fallen from the sky? Yet they survived. Who was this God who didn't have to answer for himself? Yet he kept a tight hand of expectation on his people. Bushyhead knew those who had fallen away. He understood why they had grown discouraged. He continually had to lift himself up by reading the Word. Back and forth, back and forth, the Hebrews had gone between obedience and disobedience. Yet they entered the promised land. How could Bushyhead look at the new territory as the promised land? It was a strange, inhospitable place. It was as if the Hebrews had been asked to plow the wilderness where they wandered. How much wandering there was. Bushyhead heard the cries of his people. Deliver them in this new place. Cause the land to give itself to the farmer. Let the Lord God reach down from heaven with his awful hand and give them help. Let him coax the land. Let him bring them out of their stupor.

Some mornings he could hear the groans of the people in their fields and in the poverty of their cabins. He put his hands over his ears, but still he heard their cries.

Christ had come. Christ had gone. They were under the power of Christ's resurrection. Bushyhead could preach the law of recovery. Of life.

He also could hear the conjurers singing their own song of recovery through the woods. They worked to reach the same end. Someone was haunted by someone who had died. It was an old spell to rid one of the haunting:

ghilo	*tsuniyo:hu:sv:hi*	*yidada:hnvte:ha*
someone	which died, they	if someone is thinking about you

Bushyhead stood quietly by his cabin as he felt its power strike through the leaves in the woods.

Chapter Forty-three

Knobowtee found his brother, O-ga-na-ya, in the leaves. Dried mucus caked his mouth. Dried mud was in his hair. *My brother. My brother. Was there anything I could do to stop you from this? Remember the days we fished in the creek? Remember when we were with our father? Remember the Raven Mocker? Do you want him to steal your life? I think he already has eaten your heart. Remember the days that didn't seem days? They were just there. They were our servants. They would never go away. We had them forever. The deer were ours. The bird sang for us. The sky was in our hair. The open air was there for us. We didn't think or feel. We were free. Then the shackles came. Then the clamps. We felt infringement. We felt the change. We felt the others enter our land. Before we saw them, we felt a dawning of something other than our days. We knew other days that would drive out the days we knew. Remember the weaning? Remember the hardship? Remember the dividing line that we crossed and knew when we crossed it? Remember the hard realization we were no longer boys? Now we*

have the hard land before us to sow. Our rifles have
turned into plows.

"I hated it when you killed Boudinot and the Ridges,"
Knobowtee said. "The taking of life was wrong, but it
was more than that. You killed progress. You killed
accomplishment. You killed hope for the people. If
they had— "

"I'm tired of your expediency," O-ga-na-ya interrupted with his belligerence. "All you think about is
progress," he continued. "Doesn't your God say to stamp
out our enemies?"

"The government agents and contractors deliver
inferior goods," Knobowtee answered. "We don't know
what happened to the money given to the Cherokees
for resettlement. Someone has it. Tell me who our enemies are."

In his drunkenness one evening, O-ga-na-ya set his
cabin on fire. Maritole ran through the woods to see
what was happening. She coughed from the smell of
the thick smoke.

Knobowtee followed her from the field.

"Stop, Maritole," Knobowtee caught up with her.
"There's nothing you can do."

They watched the cabin burn, fearful the fire would
catch in the trees, but it did not.

Maritole collapsed to her knees. Knobowtee lifted
her and carried her back to their cabin.

That night her labor began. The child was stillborn.

"What's wrong?" Maritole yelled at God after the
eruption of the child from within her. In the delirium
that followed, Maritole called to hold the child. But
Anna Sco-so-tah wrapped it in a blanket and laid it

outside the door. The baby was hardly formed, hardly recognizable as a baby in the candlelight of the cabin. Anna Sco-so-tah didn't want Maritole to see it, though Maritole continued to cry for it. In the fever that followed the stillbirth, Maritole called to what had been born. When she slept a moment, Anna Sco-so-tah took it outside and buried it with the others.

In the weeks that followed, Maritole struggled to believe. She knew what Reverend Bushyhead said was true, but in the hardships of the farm, she didn't believe there could be a God who let this injustice happen. Christ was stronger than any of the conqueror's spells. But it seemed as strong as the root system of field grass that was nearly impossible to break. That continued to grow with the corn and had to be plucked. Knobowtee, Willard and Watson, Anna Sco-so-tah, Aneh and her husband, Edward, and Rebekah weeded, while Maritole mourned and O-ga-na-ya struggled with the bear of his drunkenness.

"I wanted to see the baby," Maritole said to Anna Sco-so-tah angrily.

"It was dead. It didn't look like a baby. You were sick. It is buried."

"Put a fieldstone on its grave," Anna told her.

Maritole walked through the field, looking for a stone. Then she sorted through the stones they had piled along the edge of the field. She found a small stone and walked toward the baby's grave, but stopped. She saw a new stone in the graveyard by their cabin.

"Did you put a stone on the baby's grave?" Maritole asked Knobowtee that night.

"No. O-ga-na-ya put it there."

Chapter Forty-four

They had to have something other than their farms and the endless work and hardship of plowing the wilderness. The soil protested each year they broke the field for planting. Knobowtee felt the resistance as he walked behind the horse, O-ga-na-ya sometimes leading it, pulling it ahead, encouraging it as the blade struck another stone that had to be pulled from the soil, as if the horse, as well as the land, was going against the grain of their inclination. No wonder the Cherokees cried at the altar of the church. Some of it was exhaustion, not only of the body, but of the will and the spirit.

No wonder they drank.

Anna Sco-so-tah went on her hands and knees speaking to the soil, telling it to open to the corn, telling it stories. She made stick dolls and placed them at the corners of the small field.

She clucked to the soil.

If only there was some way to carry creek water to it.

O-ga-na-ya was gone again. Knobowtee needed him in the field, but he was not there.

After a week, Reverend Bushyhead cornered O-ga-na-ya near Breadtown.

"I don't want to come to your church."

"I didn't ask you to," Bushyhead said.

"I think of Stand Watie with Boudinot and the Ridges under an oak tree on the Oostanaula River signing the New Echota Treaty. What did they offer him to sign?— all the land he's got now in Honey Creek? What else goes on that we don't know about?" O-ga-na-ya kept talking, not giving Bushyhead a chance to speak. "Stand Watie carries on the Ridge and Boudinot faction, and I'm not sure you're not one of them. They sit in the front row of your church, but De-ga-ta-ga, *Stand Straight*, is bent inside. He sits on the Cherokee council. My brother, Knobowtee, should be there." O-ga-na-ya was amazed he spoke as he did. He didn't slur his words. He didn't repeat himself, or at least he didn't think he did. He sounded reasonable, rational, like someone who was sober.

"Your bitterness is choking you," Bushyhead said. "I'll perform a ceremony for you if you come to the house. I'll walk with you beside my horse. You can ride if you want."

O-ga-na-ya walked beside Bushyhead. It was then he felt his drunkenness again. He knew he had trouble walking. Sometimes he steadied himself with his hand on the horse.

Mrs. Bushyhead prepared a tea from bark. It was for the choking ceremony, which O-ga-na-ya knew.

"Drink this— it will taste bitter."

Mrs. Bushyead called the children into their house. O-ga-na-ya had not seen so many children. Some of them must be orphans.

O-ga-na-ya drank the bitter bark. Soon he bent over and threw up. He wretched and wretched.

"Your bitterness is in your vomit. You're purging yourself of it. It won't have its hands around your throat."

O-ga-na-ya felt Bushyhead's hands around his throat. He was having trouble breathing. Was he just retching again? What was Bushyhead doing? Was this part of the ceremony? O-ga-na-ya didn't think so. Would Bushyhead strangle him?

"When the bitterness comes back, tell it to leave. Think of my hands around your neck. They are the hands of bitterness." Bushyhead squeezed harder until O-ga-na-ya threw him off and stumbled away down the road. It was a windy day. Branches beat from the trees. Leaves circled around O-ga-na-ya's legs. He seemed to rise from them and walk on.

Chapter Forty-five

Part of resettlement was writing the reclamation and spoliation claims in which the Cherokees listed what they had lost.

Other lists were made when someone died:

The following schedule of property was shown to and appraised by me as belonging to the estate of Horse Fly decd., in compliance to the order of the Honble Jeffry Beck Judge of the District Court of Delaware dated the 18th Dec 1848. James Rogers.

1 cow with young calf valued at	$	7.00
1 dark cow with a yearling	$	8.00
3 Bulls 2 years old $4.50	$	13.50
1 Red pied Heaffer	$	5.00
1 Red cow & yearling	$	9.00
1 Heaffer 2 years old	$	5.00
1 Yoke of oxen	$	30.00
1 old wagon very much worn	$	17.00
1 shovel plough & gears	$	4.50
1 dog chain	$	2.50
1 hand gun[?] and other tools	$	5.00
4 ring for Britching	$	.50
1 Kettle (casting)	$	2.00
1 Side saddle (old)	$	4.50

1 hat 1.00 1 Rifle gun 5.00	$	6.00
1 Sorrel horse & bridle	$	40.00
1 grind stone (broke) 1 barrel	$	.25
Plates & coffee pot at Mr. Conner's	$	.63
1 Old steel mill (broke)	$	.50
54 head of stock hogs	$	70.00
100 bushels of corn .20	$	20.00
2 small pots at Thompson's	$	.87
1 small Beef hide	$	.50
1 table at Mr. Conners	$	1.00
Debt on Pheasen $5.00 on W. Butler 4.13	$	9.13
House & farm	$	150.00
carried over		412.38

Churn pails	$	2.00
1 Common bedstead	$	1.25
Claim against the U.S.	$	15.00
Note on Oagesquatate	$	10.00
1 Stirrip iron	$	.12
	$	500.75

The following schedule of property was shown to and appraised by me as belonging to the estate of Horse Fly dec.d in compliance to the order of the Hon.ble Jeffry Beck Judge of the District Court of Delaware dated the 18th Dec.r 1847   James Rogers

(Namely)

1 cow with a young calf valued at	$	7.00
1. Dun cow with a yearling	" "	8=00
3 Bulls 2 year olds 4.50	" "	13=50
1 Red pieded Heaffer	"	5=00
1 Red cow & yearling	"	9=00
1 Heuffer 2 years old		5=00
1 Yoke of Oxen	" "	30=00
1 old waggon very much worn	" "	17=00
1 shovel plough & gears		4=50
1 Log chain	"	2=50
1 hand saw and other tools		5=00
4 ring for Britching	"	=50
1 Kettle (casting)		2=00
1 side saddle (old)		4=50
1 hat 1.00 1 Rifle gun 5.00		6=00
1 Sorrel horse & bridle		40=00
1 gun store (broke) 1 Barrel		=25
plates & coffee pot at Mr Conner		=63
1 old steel mill (broke)		=50
54 head of stock hogs		70=00
100 bushels of corn 20 –		20=00
2 small pots at Simpsons		=87
1 small Beef hide at Butlers		=50
1 table at Mr Conners		1=00
Debt on Neasons 5. on W. Butler 4.13		9=13
House & farm		150=00
carried over –		412=38
Churn pails &c		2=00
1 common bedstead		1=25
claim against the U. S.		15=00
note on Cage Squirrels		70=00
1 strum iron		=12
		500=75

There were other lists. There were lists and lists. Document after document.

One Negro man Lorn 43 years old
One Negro woman Peggy 30 years old
One Negro woman Lydia 32 years old
One Negro boy Dobson 12 years old
One Negro boy Solomon 9 years old
One Negro boy Wiley 8 years old
One Negro boy Elic 4 years old
One Negro boy Thomas 5 years old
One Negro boy Steven 22 years old
One Negro girl Maria 6 years old
One Negro girl Josephine 1 year old
One Negro girl Dinah 1 year old

Also one mule, one jack ass, about 47 ~~y~~head [of] stock cattle more or less, one ~~yoke~~ Waggon one yo[ke] oxen, and also household & kitchen furniture[. The] guardians also promise to deliver up to me, a c[er]tain note of hand signed by Stand Watie for $200.00 made payable to the above named gentlemen for the use of the said Walter Ridge. . . .

Recd at Honey Creek Cherokee nation this 17th day
March 1852 from Rev John Huss & Mathew Moore late
of Walter Ridge decd the following named negroes and
other property herein discribed as the effects of the said
Walter Ridge decd — namely—

One negroe man Tom 43 years old
"   "   Woman Peggy 30 "   "
"   "   "   " Lydia 32 "   "
"   "   boy Dobson 12 "   "
"   "   " Solomon 9 "   "
"   "   " Wiley 8 "   "
"   "   " Elic 4 "   "
"   "   " Thomas 5 "   "
"   "   " Steven 22 "   "
"   "   girl Maria 6 "   "
~~Josephine~~ Josephine 1 "   "
"   "   " Dinah 1 "   "

Also one mule, one Jack ass about 47 head
Stock cattle more or less; one ox Waggon one yo
Oxen, and also household & kitchen furniture
guardians also promise to deliver up to me, a certain
note of hand signd by Stand Watie for $200.00 made
payable to the above named gentlemen for the use of
the said Walter Ridge, dated sometime in april 1850 twelve months
after date. All of which I receive, as agent for the
Heirs of John Ridge deceased, and Mrs Paschal, Heirs who are
to the Estate of the late Walter Ridge deceased.

Stand Watie
Agent for Sarah Paschal
& the Heirs of John R

From the Cherokee Nation Papers, reel #41, folder 4720, page 146.
Courtesy of the Western History Collections at the University of
Oklahoma.

Chapter Forty-six

Luthy and Mrs. Bushyhead were pregnant again, and Maritole had no children.

Maritole marked her reclamation claim with a stick in the dirt by the cabin step.

Mother.

Father.

Thomas somewhere in the old territory.

The baby who died on the way from the old territory.

The baby who died in the new territory before it was born.

Beulah.

Maritole lay on the ground in the cemetery of stones by the cabin. She broke into tears. She grieved for her father, her mother, her babies. Knobowtee heard her from the field when he stopped plowing a moment. He continued to plow but soon left the horse in the field and went to Maritole. He lifted her face to him and held her, rocking her in her grief.

Anna Sco-so-tah watched from the cabin, where she was making a dress for Rebekah and then for Evelene.

Chapter Forty-seven

Luthy had another boy. Now she had Mark, Ephum, Evelene, Annohee, and Thomas. It was the name Maritole would have chosen for her son, if she had a child. She might still take that name for her child.

Tanner gave Luthy a quail-bone necklace.

Reverend Bushyhead's wife had another child also.

Maritole heard a baby's cry in the creaking hinge every time they opened the door.

"I will grease it," Knobowtee said. "I hear it too."

Luthy wore her quail-bone necklace as she held her baby, Thomas. Maritole could hardly look at her. But in Maritole's opinion, Luthy seemed more humble than she had been. Maybe she was just more tired with the toil of cooking and washing.

There was a sickly boy at the orphanage. Reverend Bushyhead asked if Maritole would take it.

"It will only die. I lost Beulah. Both children I have given birth to— "

"You have Willard, Watson, and Rebekah. They're still alive. The child will die anyway of isolation. You could make his passage easier. I can't believe he is still alive."

"I could work a spell for you," Anna Sco-so-tah told Maritole. "It would help you have a child."

"No," Maritole said. "Reverend Bushyhead doesn't like spells."

"But his wife keeps having children."

"I will do it the hard way," Maritole told her. "Maybe I don't have the strength for another child as yet."

"But I hear you cry for one."

"You know Christianity and conjuring don't mix."

"There're ways to make it work."

O-ga-na-ya came home with an animal.

"What is it?" Maritole asked.

"A mule."

"Is it real?"

"There were some on the trail— at the beginning, anyway. The long-eared horse."

Yes, Maritole remembered. She had tried to put behind her all that she could from the trail.

"Where'd it come from?" Knobowtee asked.

"A trader brought it from Arkansas."

O-ga-na-ya laughed. "Some of the people were afraid and ran from them when they brought them to Breadtown."

"There're others?" Maritole asked.

Knobowtee looked at it. "What an excuse for a horse. What a misfit— just like the Cherokees alone on their farms in the new territory."

"You're not a misfit," Maritole said to Knobowtee that night in their narrow cot in the cabin. "I see you in the field and I cry for the work you do. I know your frustration. I know your frustration— " She repeated her words until they became the rhythm that connected Knobowtee to the world he tried to reach.

Chapter Forty-eight

"We didn't resettle," O-ga-na-ya said bitterly. "We had not settled in our own territory. It was already established when we were born. We don't rebuild, but build from trees and stony soil on unplowable land."

The new territory rocked as if it was a wagon still jolting over the ground. Disturbance came from within and without. Such an upheaval drove things outward that usually stayed buried, but it moved rocks, tore down boundaries. Everything ran loose. The political upheaval. The new division over slaves— keep them, let them go. Scandals. Schisms. Maritole looking one way, Knobowtee another. And O-ga-na-ya even another way from Knobowtee. There were divisions from the old settlement to the new. There was the Kee-too-wah Society. The pile of sticks for their fire. Holy men, renegades, night runners, mysterious happenings, and the farmers— the farmers— the farmers. And all the conjuring magic. The Cherokee words struggling with the English. The two languages having to live side by side. The whine of a mosquito hovering near the ear.

It was not what Knobowtee would have chosen first, he decided, tired of the hardship of farming. He would have been a deer hunter, a conjurer, a traveler, a leader, anything but a farmer with a wife who had hurt him. But she was there. She was holding on. She was coping. She was trying to cook with nothing. She was stable. Some wives had gone crazy, or sat in the yard looking at a tree trunk, unable to move. Or left their children without direction— they were running everywhere and would never get anywhere in this world with a mosquito heart its core.

If the Cherokees could hold their own through hardship— if they didn't succumb and go under— if they kept that sense of who they were though the U.S. government scorned them, gave them the worst it had— they could survive—

"Keep your head above water," Anna Sco-so-tah cackled, and Maritole pictured the wide eye of the horse crossing the Hiwassee River that she had seen at the beginning of their journey.

"I remember you in the Hiwassee helping that old man across the water as we started on the removal trail," Maritole told Knobowtee.

Knobowtee remembered the cold water. He saw a brightness in Maritole's eyes that he had not seen in a long time. As he looked at her that day, he felt something inside him toward her thaw.

Reverend Bushyhead worked to establish civilization. But Knobowtee and Maritole worked to establish their daily lives.

Chapter Forty-nine

J esse Bushyhead, Oo-no-du-tu, had been born in Cleveland, Tennessee, Meigs County, on September 5, 1804. He was the son of John and Nancy Foreman Bushyhead. He was the husband of Elsie Wilkenson. He was the father of five children, with another on the way.

On December 19, 1829, the Georgia legislature had passed an act that appropriated a large area of the Cherokee Nation. Other states had followed. Bushyhead had been incarcerated in the stockade near Camp Hetzel, near Cleveland, Tennessee. He had been released. Then it was nearly ten years before the confusion of the roundup, when soldiers once again took Cherokees to the stockades. He remembered the haphazard division of the Cherokees into detachments. Sometimes starting one way, joining with another group from another place, adding groups, not knowing who they were, sharing the trail with strangers, even though they were also Cherokees.

He remembered when a nearby county, Rhea, had nearly doubled in size with the annexation of part of the Cherokee Nation. He remembered the rows of hills and mountains they had left. Sometimes he thought they called to him. He thought of the streams and creeks. He remembered the dried leaves on the forest floor, the underbrush, the fog.

He could almost hear the moccasins of a runner through the woods. The sound of the first splots of rain. Birds talking. A deer running on its hind legs. It was a sign that things would change.

The settlers annexed their country, the yellow red and yellow brown soil, the fir trees and oaks, words heard in the streams, the gullies and ravines.

Bushyhead remembered when civilization was a few wagon ruts and footpaths in the woods.

When he had to leave Meigs County, he remembered walking away, looking back every few steps until the rows of hills grew paler in the distance. He remembered his cabin in the clearing in the pines. The hills and mountains they had left called to him. The streams and creeks of Meigs County. Dried leaves on the forest floor. The underbrush. The morning fog from the river with its lowlands. He remembered logs fallen on the floor of the woods. Felled logs. Axes for cutting trees. Planes for plank flooring.

What magic, what spells could lift their cabins from nothing?

He tried to pull his congregation along. He tried to carry them in his prayers. But their needs were more than he ever could meet. He felt his words were a few small kernels in a large field of corn.

The Cherokees had marched west. They had been afraid of marching west, the direction of death, but the west was still far ahead of them in the distance. Would the conjurers' warnings and superstitions always be with him, or would he find a way to put them to rest?

Chapter Fifty

Knobowtee worked in the field digging fieldstones. It reminded him of digging graves on the removal trail. He knew Maritole thought of her parents, and the baby they had lost on the trail when she heard the sound of his shovel, but he didn't know how to dig without the noise of the shovel hitting rock. Removing stones buried in the soil was hard work.

The stones were for healing. Knobowtee remembered the stone man story. Nun'yunu'wi had arrived in the new territory. That was sure. His stones were everywhere. How were the stones they put on graves healing? They were healing for those who died, who had gone to the other world and were no longer sick or suffering. But how were they healing for those who lived? The rocks they used for graves were a reminder that suffering didn't last forever, but would come to an end. Knobowtee longed at times for the end, but he would not give up. He heard Anna Sco-so-tah pounding corn with her pestle. Maybe the hardships were pounding them into cornmeal. Maybe they were being made something he could not yet understand.

The birds spoke to Knobowtee, not in words, but

the song— he listened to the stroke of sound on the light. Willard and Watson saw Knobowtee looking at the sky, and they did too. Knobowtee had become a dreamer. He saw a wide land with nothing on it. Then rain and cold and fire came upon it— and something else that could not be seen. The field rose with corn and retreated in winter. It advanced with crops again the next spring. Discouragement was the enemy. Knobowtee fought against it as he dreamed. He didn't know if he was awake or if he had fallen asleep in the field as he dug. Knobowtee felt his father plowing beside him in the field. But his father had not farmed. He had not plowed. How would he know what to do? Knobowtee told him he could go back to the other world, where he could be a hunter.

Knobowtee was part of the new nation. Willard and Watson were too. Tanner and his family. Edward and his. They were a nation of makers, of inventors. The Cherokees had invented an alphabet, a syllabary, actually, with written characters for sounds in the Cherokee language. The Cherokees were making their farms. They were making their lives. Not just repeating chants, but making them up on their own, mixing them with prayers.

Knobowtee saw Maritole sweeping out the cabin. In the dust were dead flies, dried pieces of mud, spiders, leaves. The sound of field mice burrowing under the cabin at night. An owl in the tree near the cabin answering another owl on the other side of the field. A crane by the creek in the morning. One squirrel scolding another. The birds wild with noise. Watson, when he had an earache, held his hands to his ears when he walked with Maritole from the creek.

They were not alone on the earth, but were part of a new nation, obeying a new name over them.

Chapter Fifty-one

The conjurers built their cabins in the woods of the new territory. They kept their families around them. They dug rocks from their soil. They realigned the chants and ceremonies that had accompanied them on the removal trail. They had brought their ways with them. Diviners asked why the trail had happened? Could they have done something? Was there a ceremony they could have performed to drive the intruders away? No, they had tried. They had tried. Some things were bigger than magic, some of the people said. No, it was part of their magic to move. To split. To retrieve. To rethink.

In the aftermath of the removal, the conjurers wanted the same thing the Christians wanted. If only the church would understand, they could work together. They both wanted healing and restoration for the Cherokees. The conjurers went to the water for cleansing from the hurt of the trail. The Christians went to the water for baptism. The water was where they met.

In the fields, the conjurers turned the stones in their hands, asking them to move, repeating phrases to make

paths for them to the edges of their fields. The stones
had voices. What were they saying? They did not want
to move. Yes, the conjurers understood that. They kept
turning the stones in their hands as they dug them from
the ground, telling them they did not come intention-
ally to move them from their place, but had themselves
been removed.

ha:niyu   *ha:niyu*
get out of the way!   get out of the way!

sge?   *odahli*   *tsugv:yiyi*
listen   mountain   at first

iyv:dvgwo   *ni:dodv:gwadunvhi*
far, just   over there, I arose from

ha   *nv:ya*   *igahvshi*
ha   rock   sayer

nv:do   *dunanu:gotsv:hi*   *ha*   *nv:no:hi*   *aye:hliyu*
sun   earliest rising   ha   pathways   middle, very

duda:n(v)do?   *doduligv:haseyasvli:ga*
soul, his   he has just come to chop up

The conjurers told the rocks to move aside as they
plowed.

    The conjurers invoked their spells as they broke
their way into the new territory— as they spoke their
way into the new territory— rendering their words in
accordance with the old ways. They felled the trees,
plowed the soil, rebuilt. They had carried the knowledge that had made their way since the beginning.

The birds were always talking all at once. The stones and the stones and the stones were speaking. They were trying to outspeak the birds. Everything had wings. Even the field. Even the fieldstones. The conjurers felt the updraft of their words. They felt the flying aside of the sky.

After plowing all day, often the conjurers were called to cabins, and tents of tarp, and sometimes only blankets tied to trees and staked to the ground. The families heard witches pass on the road at night. They called the conjurers to work their ceremonies and ward off whatever bothered them. The conjurers felt the stirring of the Cherokees' fears and anger and anguish and ventings that rumbled the night air. At night, the air was as full of sounds as it was of birdsong in the day.

The conjurers were called to stabilize the weather.

They were called to invoke the hard shell of the turtle for resilience. They were called to call up everything they knew.

They worked with their remade language, calling it from its old form, rethinking it, recreating it— Thought Energy— that's what conjuring was. That's why it was powerful. Their spirit of their words smoldered underground like the Kee-too-wah fire they had brought from the old territory.

The conjurers' words were not made as a conduit for another, such as the Bible work of Jesse Bushyhead and Evan Jones. It was not a reflection of another, but a determiner of itself, of how things had been and would continue to be.

By a word, a conjurer could remove stones from his field. For the Christians, it was their God who did things for them, though the conjurers saw Christians sweating as though they themselves removed the stones from their fields.

Chapter Fifty-two

Bushyhead looked over his list again at his house at Pleasant Hill. How hopeless it seemed when they had nothing. But making a list helped establish his thoughts. He needed to list. Listing was a holy act, he thought as he sat near his family busy in their cabin.

Instead of making of list of what he needed, he began to make a list of what he heard. What he thought. Bits of conversation. Names he remembered. He should be working on his sermon notes on how to obey the God who had shuffled their world. But he continued with his lists. He had a swarm of memories like insects. If he lost sight of the whole, if it was too much for him to look at, he had the fragments.

They were from Ooltewah. A place between Cleveland and Chattanooga.

Sound carries light.

A porch or porch roof. A smooth wide-plank floor.

How many factions rubbing against one another?

Daniel McCoy.

John Bell and Joseph Lynch owned two stables.

Hewn logs. Plank floor. Puncheon floor— the logs split lengthwise.

The First Council House in New Echota.

A log house. Dog-trot style. A long porch with an opening in the middle of the house, a walk-through. The walls with dovetailed joints.

Smokehouse. Corncrib. Barn.

Two short posts in a V-shape driven in the ground at intervals to hold the saplings stretched between them.

Alexander McCoy, a Cherokee, operated the ferry from 1819 to 1835.

The Boudinots also had a turkey house.

Gourds. Jugs. Candle molds. Iron. Broom. Masks. Anvil. Auger. Spindle and weaving loom. River-cane blowgun. Mortar and pestle to grind corn.

The posts of the house sat on stones.

They gathered rocks for the chimney.

Samuel Worcester had closets in his house.

George Lowrey, Deputy and Principal Chief.

John Ross, Major Ridge, Spokesmen of the Council.

John Ridge, David Vann, and Joseph Vann, 1829 Council.

Circuit court and Supreme Court in New Echota.

The two house legislatures became three like the U.S. government.

Worcester was minister and postmaster at the mission.

William Tarvin, postmaster, arrived in 1829.

The tavern was built on the federal road.

What was the blacksmith's name?

How far did we walk today?

How far did we plow?

Knobowtee and Maritole rode the mule to the mission for the sickly child, whom they took back to their farm. Bushyhead watched them as they left. Knobowtee leading the mule, Maritole riding with the child on her lap.

How did Maritole and Knobowtee get in his detachment? Weren't they from North Carolina? Bushyhead couldn't remember. Maybe they had become separated from their own group. Maybe some of his Tennessee people had been mixed with other groups.

Let it go. Let it go, he told himself. There were too many other things to think about.

Chapter Fifty-three

Hervey Upham, an experienced printer, came to the mission to help with Bushyhead's vision of a newspaper. The press provided by the missionary board was an upgrade from the old cast-iron press with spiral springs to hold the type plates in New Echota. For inking, they had used deerskin balls stuffed with wool. Two of the printers had married the sisters of Elias Boudinot, who had been murdered.

"What happened to the metal type plates from the printing press in the Phoenix office?"

"We had to leave them behind," Bushyhead said. "The militia wreaked havoc with them too."

"What happened to them? No one moving in could read them."

"I'm sure they were thrown out on the ground. Maybe someone dug a hole and buried the type plates. Our words will be left in the soil of the old territory. Our language will always be there."

Chapter Fifty-four

BAPTIST MISSIONARY MAGAZINE, VOL. 27, NO. 7 (JULY 1847):

The translation of the New Testament into Cherokee is completed, together with the book of Genesis. The 1st and 2nd Thessalonians, Titus and Philemon were about to be put to press, 5000 copies in tract form, and 5000 for the New Testament edition. Twelve numbers of the Messenger *have been printed, and about 200 copies bound for sale and distribution.*

Cherokees—Rev. E. Jones, Rev. W. P. Upham, teacher, Mr H. Upham, printer, and their wives.
Flint—Lewis Downing, native preacher. 3 out-stations
Taquohee—Tanenole, native preacher
Dsyohee—Dsulaskee, native preacher
Delaware—John Wickliffe, Oganiah, native preachers. 2 out-stations

5 stations and 5 out-stations; 2 preachers; 1 teacher, 1 printer; 3 female assistants; 5 native preachers.

*Mrs. E. S. Morse, recently of the mission, has been trans-
ferred to Ottawa station of the Shawanoe Mission. Miss S.
H. Hibbard is now resident in the States. The occasion of
their removal from the Cherokees' country, as intimated in
our last report, was the increased number of the Cherokees'
national schools, rendering the employment of female missionary teachers unnecessary. The health of Miss Hibbard,
which had been impaired, the Committee have been happy
to learn is fully restored. The removal of Mr. W. P. Upham
from Taquohee to Cherokee has resulted partly from the
superior importance of the school department at the latter
place, as respects both the number and character of the
pupils, and partly from the faculties thereby secured to Mr.
Upham in preaching to the Cherokees. At Taquohee his
labors as a preacher had for months been almost nominal
for want of an interpreter. At Cherokee he will also take the
pastoral charge of a church about to be constituted there,
and will have frequent opportunities for forming acquain-
tance with the native preachers and others who resort
thither, and for imparting to them counsel and instruction.
His residence at Taquohee the past three years has been
acceptable and profitable to the people, and his departure
appears to have been to them an occasion of deep regret. It
should be noted here that the population had greatly
decreased in consequence of the late civil disturbances, and
the national school was liable to be discontinued at any
time, the number of pupils being less than twenty-five.*

*In regard to the success of evangelical efforts among the
people, we have less to report than in some preceding years,
owing in part to the agitated state of society during the last
twelve or eighteen months. Many of the religious meetings
however have been well attended, and a few have been
added to the churches by baptism. The number of additions*

in the months from April to December inclusively is reported fourteen; and there are others, at all the places of stated preaching, who give serious attention to the word. In several neighborhoods houses for religious worship have been lately built; one at Verdigris, twenty feet by twenty-three; Grand River, one, twenty-six by twenty-two; and one at Choi Stoi, on Spring Creek, about twenty feet square; making in all about ten log buildings for the accommodation of worshippers.

Chapter Fifty-five

Maritole asked Knobowtee to be baptized with her. She asked him to marry her in the church. A simple service with Reverend Bushyhead. It could be done in private. They would go to the creek by themselves for the baptism. They could even stand by a tree and Bushyhead would read the Christian marriage service. They didn't have to be in the church. They could say their marriage vows anywhere. They could forgive one another.

What a rough road forgiveness was. What a muddy field. You couldn't walk away from it clean. Forgiveness stuck to you. Or the process of forgiveness. It plowed a field. It made way for a crop.

Chapter Fifty-six

"How could they go to the afterlife with nothing? How could they go to the unknown? They had to give themselves up to it. The Christian went to heaven that was full of cornfields. The conjurers went to their place they thought was the transformation of their magic." Reverend Bushyhead preached the funeral of Quaty Lewis after church one Sunday. Another funeral followed hers.

Afterward, he traveled to the creek with Knobowtee, Maritole, Willard, Watson, Anna Sco-so-tah, and the sick child. Rebekah was with Aneh and Edward and their children. Reverend Bushyhead spoke about the hardships they faced. The childlessness of Maritole was a bear. The bear also had Knobowtee in its mouth. Faith was a bear that Bushyhead wore like a tunic. He would not take it off. Others belonged to conjuring. They were not bound by his circumstances but believed they could surround themselves with magic.

"There is hope in the Christian God. There also is hope in the spells and the magic of words. The Christian world is settled. It is written in a book that is alive," Bushyhead said. "It has the power of spells. It is from the spell binder himself, God. It is a person, Jesus Christ. That is power I choose," Bushyhead kept talking. He was aware of the odd baptismal service he was performing for Knobowtee, Maritole, Anna Sco-so-tah, Rebekah and the two boys, and the sick child from whom breath was nearly gone. Was he talking or merely thinking? He was unsure of what he was doing, but he knew he was doing something. The powers were separate trails. They were not the same. Though they both were magic. One was the counterfeit of the other. Knobowtee had to choose which road he wanted to walk, because they led to different places.

"Do not be deceived," Bushyhead told him. "The conjurers use a lively power. It can't be denied. We all have seen it. The Christian faith is not so obvious." It was another bear they pushed.

"Which one are you, Anna Sco-so-tah?" Bushyhead turned to her suddenly.

"I've decided to be a Christian," she answered, startled. "I've been acting like one, haven't I? Aren't I always in your church?"

"You have to be one or the other. You can't be both."

"I thought it was possible."

"You sound Christian, but I hear a conjurer's spell." Reverend Bushyhead put his hands on Anna Sco-so-tah's head. In a loud voice, he called for indecision to disappear. He asked that she separate herself. When he called for the separation, she fell crying to her knees in the shallow edge of the creek. She couldn't tell if it was Christian force or a conjurer's spell.

Reverend Bushyhead baptized the six of them in the water where they stood.

Edward didn't want their children baptized. It didn't seem to matter to Aneh.

Afterward, Maritole and Knobowtee repeated the marriage vows.

It was late that evening when Reverend Bushyhead returned to his cabin.

Chapter Fifty-seven

Maritole tried to hold the sickly child to this world, but he died.

Bushyhead rode to their farm for a service. Tanner, Luthy, and their children came from their adjoining farm. Aneh, Edward, and their children came from theirs. O-ga-na-ya arrived late, looking disheveled. Bushyhead blessed the burial plot by the cabin.

The following Sunday, Bushyhead told a story in the Cherokee way.

Long ago at a Green Corn dance, a dog began howling. He told the man to build a house that would float on water. The man, his wife, children, and the dog went into the house and soon the rain began. It rained seven days and drowned the whole world.

The conjurers were working their magic. The ministers were praying for rain. The thin rows of corn were stunted by drought. They told stories. Stories made the world tolerable. Well, not tolerable, because the corn was withering in the field, but stories gave them something other than what they had at the time. Rain would come again. Rain so hard they would pray it stop.

In the time of hunger, they thought of pies, bread, beef, fowl, and corn.

gu   wi   si   da   he.

Knobowtee knew a contingent went to Washington to tell them of the hardship of Cherokee resettlement. Why didn't they bring Washington to Indian Territory to show them?

The Cherokees would continue to face disorder, shootings, woundings, accidents, upheaval within themselves as well as in the new territory. Knobowtee and O-ga-na-ya felt the division and turbulence of the Cherokees. Sometimes the brothers worked against themselves. What could Knobowtee do to bring O-ga-na-ya into alignment before he got into trouble from which he could not escape? That's what they needed. To feel in alignment with the old order.

And now there was a new disorder. The disruption of politics. The abolitionists, the white soldiers and Pins, the traditionals, the conservatives, the Cherokees for the north called Kee-too-wah. Then there were the mixed-bloods, the ones who took up the new way. How many more fractures would there be?

A Cherokee was free. A Cherokee was a servant. There was opposition. Contradiction. All of it, a howling dog who began to speak of a flood.

Get rid of superstitious beliefs. They were free in Christ, Bushyhead preached.

Yet they were slaves to him also.

Bushyhead worked to educate, to tame, to Christianize, to bring into the light.

The hardest part was the move from communal to individual responsibility.

Knobowtee knew they would prevail in their poverty if they worked as a group. What a change from the large communal fields where everyone worked, to small plots over which the single farmer had responsibility. It was more than one man could accommodate.

Indolence was an enemy. The inability to get a handle. To be overcome by the largeness of the situation. Indolence, it seemed to Knobowtee and O-ga-na-ya, was justified. It was a response suitable to the circumstance. They were overpowered by the new land, by its indolence in not taking the plow, the seed. It was the indolence of the sky not to provide the clouds needed for rain. It withheld its efforts. Or it let out too much rain and drowned the young crop. The Cherokees were just reflecting their situation. They were in a reciprocity to the land.

Debt, discouragement, doubt, hopelessness, actually, when they were overwhelmed— when they were small against the largeness against them.

Bushyhead would remind them of David, with his stone against Goliath. He would remind them of Israel, outnumbered in their journeys. He would preach about bread from heaven, manna, but stopped as he realized again that Indian Territory was not the promised land.

Their lessons were their fragile lives. The daily need for food, for subsistence. It was not fair. This daily need with no way to meet it. Who was this God in the sky who gave men stomachs without a way to fill them? They boiled bark. They killed small animals. They looked for plants, for weeds. The hunger for bread. For bread. For bread. The women always asking the men for what they could not provide. How irritating women were. Did they know how hard they were to live with?

O-ga-na-ya's quick temper flared. His tendency to retaliate before thinking.

The Cherokees were broken off from the whole and made to grip the small part that they were alone.

Bushyhead had felt crazed at times. He lived in fragments. But he kept track of them. Knowing somehow they would come together again.

Chapter Fifty-eight

BAPTIST MISSIONARY MAGAZINE, VOL. 30, NO. 1 (JANUARY 1850):

Under a deep sense of unworthiness, and of the rich mercies of God continued to us through our blessed Redeemer, I beg leave to communicate some of the instances of his goodness.

Though the seasons have for several months been very unfavorable, on account of the severity of weather in early spring, and a succession of freshets until a few days ago; very few of our meetings have been disappointing. Our native brethren have evinced their devotedness to the cause of Christ by swimming rivers, wading swamps, and riding through storms of sleet, snow and rain, to meet their appointments. The affectionate, prompt and efficient cooperation of these brethren is to me matter of sincere gratitude; nor can I express in adequate terms the praise due to the God of all grace, for the influences of his Holy Spirit; which have attended the word preached, and which, I trust, has made it the power of God unto salvation to many souls.

I should be glad to give an account of a number of interesting meetings, which have been blessed with gracious tokens of the divine presence; wounding the hearts of sinners, and leading them to the blood of Christ. At present, I only send you the results:— the hopeful conversion of seventy-seven precious souls, and their baptism on a profession of their faith in the atoning Savior.

Mr. Jones writes again, Sept. 5

We have had a meeting at Flint, which commenced Thursday last, Aug. 30th and continued four days. Religious exercises commenced Thursday evening, and continued Friday all day. At night while urging each Christian present to use some effort to bring sinners to Christ, much solemnity prevailed, and the members agreed to use their influence and their prayers to promote the conversion of sinners during the present meeting. Saturday morning, at early prayer meeting, while enlarging on the same topic, pressing on them the necessity of Christians making efforts beyond self, in union with Christ, for the benefit of others, they were much affected, and the members agreed to meet for a short time immediately after breakfast. The mission cause was then commended to their sympathies, prayers, and labors. The glorious opening in France and China were urged as motives to action. There was much affectionate feeling manifested, and a willingness expressed to do what they could. But here we greatly need the help of an active, pious brother, to train and encourage the Cherokee members in these duties.

At night, there was quite a movement among sinners present. Good attention had been given during the day; and now on invitation to the anxious, about fifty came up, many of them deeply affected. Much conversation was had with them, mingled with exhortation and prayer. Deep serious-ness prevailed. A temporary shade, about eighty feet by thirty, was filled with people.

On the Sabbath, after the principal morning exercises, brother Downing and myself had the happiness to bury in baptism, on a profession of their faith in Christ, nine Cherokees; one male and eight females. Two of them were quite aged women and one little girl about ten years old. Much solemnity prevailed among several hundred spectators to witness the administration of the ordinance.

The sacrament of the Lord's Supper was then administered by brethren Oganiah and Tanenole.

We reached home, with a number of our brethren and sisters from a distance, in time for the monthly concert. This was also a good season. I addressed the meeting at some length. Br. Downing spoke a little with unction, but was so overpowered that he could not proceed. His prayer was like the broken and contrite heart, uttering its humble plea in sighs that God can hear. The congregation was melted down, and wept too. Brother Tanenole was scarcely less affected, while he prayed, with humble urgency, for the outpouring of the Holy Spirit on ourselves and on the world. I think there were not many present who did not feel more or less impressed with the sacredness of the presence of God.

Tuesday morning before departing of our distant friends, we had a little conference meeting. Br. Oganiah reminded us of the goodness of God, and the gracious and signal answers to prayer we had experienced in past years, when all the members of the church united to pray for a blessing on our feeble labors, and the conversion of sinners commenced and continued from year to year, so that for years, few Sabbaths passed without some sinners professing their faith in the Savior's blood.

Br. Tanenole mentioned an incident connected with the four days meeting at Taquohee last year, which greatly affected us all. The brethren and sisters had labored hard to have cabins and provisions ready for the meeting. Every thing was ready but meal. They had sent to all the mills they knew of, within twenty miles; but on account of the drought had entirely failed to get grinding done. They were greatly distressed. Within four days of the meeting all was dark. At last, they remembered to lay the matter before him. The next day they received information that they could get all they wanted within five miles. So they were ready for the meeting in good season; in addition to which, their souls were prepared to receive and to relish the bread that cometh down from heaven.

Before separating, we all engaged to devote some time every day, until the four days meeting at Delaware Town on the 13th inst., to pray for the gracious presence of the Spirit of God on that occasion.

Chapter Fifty-nine

Fort Gibson received shovels for digging wells. Reverend Bushyhead announced it in church one Sunday. The following week, Knobowtee called a conjurer. It was the only time Maritole would allow one in their field. Knobowtee and Tanner had to make sure water would be at the bottom of the hole they would dig. They asked the conjurer to find water between the adjoining farms. That way they only would have to dig and maintain one well.

The conjurer drummed in the field. He rattled his gourd. He walked one way over the ground. He walked another. Water was there. Where was it expedient to dig? Maritole took Willard, Watson, and Rebekah into the cabin. She closed the door. Anna Sco-so-tah sat with her. They could hear the conjurer at work. They could hear the old language and the old magic of that language. She could feel the cabin change and move to its power. Why was it frightening? It worked against the magic she knew Bushyhead preached. The light and the light. How could they be the same? But the conjurer had power. Something old broke loose in Maritole and she cried at the table. The children were playing in the corner and didn't see her. They did not seem to be aware of the conjurer's noise. They would not know the old world that was subsumed by the new. There would be rivulets of it. There would be an underground song of it. There would be those who would carry the old tradition above ground.

For a moment Maritole was in the world she had known as a child— when she was with her father and mother at the festivals after harvesting corn. She heard the old world move in the conjurer's song. It was the world the Cherokees created with their singing. It threaded through her consciousness. It was an enormous world from which their first, pitiful stomp dance in the new territory was only a shadow, something like the moon when it was a sliver in the night sky. Maritole looked at the dirt on her hands and under her fingernails. It was the dirt of the new territory. She pulled the old thread loose and felt the momentary sting. There was a spot of blood where she had pulled the small piece of skin from her finger by the nail. For one moment, she touched the world she was leaving behind. *Good-bye. Good-bye. You were all to me. But I give up remembering. Now I help plow the new field. You only get in the way. Move over*— Maritole pushed the rump of the bear. It left the cabin, for that moment anyway.

O-ga-na-ya would rebuild the cabin he had burned. He would stop living with the trees. There were times he dreamed of the three men he had killed. There were times he heard their families cry. There were times he heard the whole Cherokee Nation mourn for the actions of its people. Maritole had seen O-ga-na-ya wash at the creek in winter in a way that sought cleansing. If he wasn't drinking, he was working to recover from alcohol.

Maritole went to the field as the conjurer finished. Maybe he would point to her and say a child would come to her. Maybe he would use his divining stones and say she would have a baby. But he just looked at her. Maybe he wasn't the kind of conjurer who knew all things.

The men dug the well a piece at a time. Maritole dug also. Anna Sco-so-tah prayed over the hole down to the water. Willard and Watson carried dirt away from the hole in a little travois O-ga-na-ya made. They took it to a shallow place at the far edge of the field.

Maritole gathered the stones to line the well. Maybe they were part of the stone man who had come to devour the lives of the Cherokees, yet when they overcame him, he left healing stones for them.

She saved bark for the bucket they would make to pull the water from the ground. There would not be all those trips to the creek for water. There would not be all that carrying.

The smell of earth was upon them in the cabin. They brought it in with them from digging the well. The cabin smelled like it was underground. Maybe it would be their grave as they dug down and down into the earth. Yes, it was a kind of death. But water would come from the hole. It would come out of their own land. Out of it their lives would return.

Afterword

Pushing the Bear, the 1838–1839 Cherokee Trail of Tears

I have known about the Trail of Tears since I was a girl and we visited my Cherokee relatives in north-western Arkansas. My mother was of English and German descent. My father was an undocumented Cherokee, because his grandfather was not in Indian Territory at the time of the Dawes Rolls. I grew up with the maternal side of my family. Once in a while, we made visits to my father's people. Something not talked about was there. Attention was paid to ripples on a lake. The clouds. The leaves. The way something moved was taken notice of. When I moved to Oklahoma after college, I began to feel again the presence of that unknown history. I remember driving to Tahlequah, Oklahoma, when I lived in Tulsa, to see an outdoor presentation of the Trail of Tears at the Cherokee Heritage Museum. Afterward, I visited research libraries and eventually drove the nine hundred miles of the trail, from New Echota, Georgia, to Fort Gibson, Oklahoma, which was called Indian Territory at the time.

I think it was in passing over the land that I began to hear the voices of the people in my imagination and began to think how they could fit together in a book. I am interested in giving voice to history. It takes many voices to tell the story of a nation. That's why there are so many people talking in the first novel, *Pushing the Bear: The Removal Trail.* In the end, the readers should not try to track the individuals as much as just listen to the voices washing over them. The characters are speaking as a tribe. Dan Taylor, professor at Bethel University in St. Paul, Minnesota, called the point of view "communal first-person." The broken narrator, or the narrator broken into many parts or persons, serves another purpose besides the tribal "many speaking as one." Dividing the narration kept the story from weighing on one character alone. In other words, the multiple narrators distribute the burden of the Trail of Tears. For this reason, the book about the removal trail is difficult to get through at times. But the novel about the removal trail uses a different world-view: the one-as-all, as opposed to Western culture's emphasis on the individual. A nation is as strong as the diversity of its people, though often it is discomforting to look into a culture that is not your own.

I suppose the novel could be called *fictional, historical nonfiction.* There are known events: the Cherokees marched about ten miles a day, the line of Cherokees in the beginning was ten miles long, no one knows what happened to the money the government paid the Cherokees for removal, one-fourth died on the trail (as did most on all the westward trails in the early days, such as the Oregon, Santa Fe, and California trails, through sickness, accident, and harsh elements).

As I researched the Trail of Tears, I found information about events before and after the trail, and there was a line linking the two—"and they walked 900 miles." Wait, I thought, that is what I wanted to know—the spirit, the emotional journey, the heart-beat during the march.

Several years ago at a conference, after I gave a talk, Marion Oettinger, Curator of the San Antonio Museum of Art, told me he would send me a book he had had for thirty years, *The Nineteenth Annual Report of the Bureau of American Ethnology to the Secretary of the Smithsonian Institution, Part I, 1897–98,* by J. W. Powell, published by the Washington Printing Office in 1900. It was a large, heavy old book, just over five hundred pages long. I kept it in my office at Macalester College until after I retired and moved to Kansas. Five years later, when I was thinking about continuing the story of the Cherokees, I opened the book and began the story of resettlement in the new territory: *Pushing the Bear: After the Trail of Tears.*

When I began work on this second novel, the question was, what was it like to begin again from nothing?

There are three major themes in both books: political issues (a few chiefs signed away the land without agreement from the rest), religion (Christianity vs. the conjurers), and gender (uprooting is usually more difficult on the men; the women continue to prepare the meals and take care of the children—thus their lives do not change as radically).

In *Pushing the Bear: The Removal Trail,* there are historical voices mixed with those of fictional characters. There are fictional conversations attributed to real characters (Chief John Ross in President Andrew Jackson's office, for instance, and Reverend Bushyhead, for another). There are real historical happenings attributed to fictional characters.

In *Pushing the Bear: After the Trail of Tears*, I worked mainly with the fictional characters. The notable exceptions are Reverend Bushyhead, buried in the Old Mission cemetery in Westville, Oklahoma, just northwest of Tahlequah, and Reverend Evan Jones, whose letters I used.

I also traveled to the Baptist National Archives in Nashville, Tennessee, and read through the *Baptist Missionary Magazines*, because I was interested in the impact of Christianity on the Cherokees. I was amazed at the way the letters departed from what I knew of the hardships of the farmers' lives. At first, I separated the missionary letters from the text of the book, placing them at the end because they worked against the story. But as I continued to work on the novel, I decided to use the separate layers, structuring their overlay with abutment against each other.

As I continued writing, the book came to me in two different ways.

I saw it as an image of microfilm when reading the reclamation claims at the Oklahoma Historical Society.

I also saw it as an old black-and-white photograph—the kind made by a camera that may have been called *pinhole*, in which the edges of the photo were blurred but, in the center, a small image of clarity.

It was an image that held the Cherokee resettlement in Indian Territory as they worked to make a clearing in the trees for their field. The edges of their lives were in darkness, with only, once in a while, a brief spot of light.

This book is about what happened to the characters after they arrived in the new territory. Instead of a novel broken into many voices, it is one narrator speaking in a *daguerreotype* style of writing. Or in a historical voice sometimes brief as microfilm, with blurred or obliterated parts that have disappeared with time. I wanted to present the feel of the limited evidence we have of the first few years after the arrival.

William Hagen, Oklahoma Baptist University, who led library discussions in Oklahoma of the first book, told me that he received the suggestion that a list of characters should have been included. At various readings I heard the same comments, so I list them here in this later book as a memorial to the earlier characters.

CHARACTERS IN *PUSHING THE BEAR: THE REMOVAL TRAIL*

Maritole, a young Cherokee woman
Knobowtee, her husband
Maritole's father, died at the end of the removal trail
Maritole's mother, died at the beginning of the trail and was buried on the Cumberland Mountain at the beginning of the journey
Maritole's baby, died with Maritole's mother and was buried with her
Tanner and Luthy, Maritole's brother and sister-in-law and their young boys, Mark and Ephum
Thomas, Maritole's and Tanner's younger brother who escaped into the North Carolina Mountains—he does not appear in the novel
O-ga-na-ya, Knobowtee's brother
Knobowtee's mother, died on the trail
Aneh, Knobowtee's sister

A group of older women:
Anna Sco-so-tah
Quaty Lewis
Lacey Woodard

The Widow Teehee, died on the trail
Kee-un-e-ca, died on the trail
Mrs. Young Turkey, died at the end of the trail

A group of older men:
War Club, an old man
Kinchow, Anna's neighbor, died on the trail
Wah-ke-cha
Voices as they Walked, Voices in the Dark

Nonfictional characters:
John Ross, chief of the Cherokee nation
Reverend Bushyhead, a Cherokee minister
Reverend Evan Jones, a white minister
Reverend Mackenzie
The Soldiers
The Light Horse Guard
J. H. Hetzel, a physician at Rattlesnake Springs
A White Traveler from Maine
Terrapin Head
Alotohee
Kakowih
Tannoswech
Wauskulta Claim for Spoliation
Sally Bee Hunter, Claim for Spoliation
Willy Drowning Bear, Claim for Spoliation
Elizabeth Cooper, Claim for Spoliation
Sophia Sawyer
James Mooney's writings
A Government Teamster's Journal

Characters that appear only once:
Gelest, an old woman who turned into a deer
Bird Doublehead

William Holland, trading-post owner
Kehtohih
A Holy Man
Him-Who-We-See-the-Bones-of-His-Hand
The Basket Maker
Ella Rogers

As with my other books of historical narrative, whether for the characters in *Pushing the Bear: The Trail of Tears,* or Sacajawea on the Lewis and Clark Expedition in *Stone Heart,* or Kateri Tekakwitha, a seventeenth-century Mohawk converted by the Jesuits in *The Reason for Crows,* or the late nineteenth-century Ghost Dancers at Walker Lake in northwestern Nevada in *The Dance Partner,* I drove to the place where the history took place. For this particular book, I made several trips to northeastern Oklahoma in search of *voice,* which has become a part of my writing process. It was in standing on the ground at Fort Gibson, the arrival point, and picking up the rock that appears below, that I began to place a created voice into a historical narrative.

Works Consulted

Justice, Daniel Heath. *Our Five Survives the Storm: A Cherokee Literary History*. Minneapolis: University of Minnesota Press, 2006.

McLoughlin, William G. *After the Trail of Tears: The Cherokees' Struggle for Sovereighty, 1839–1880*. Chapel Hill: University of North Carolina Press, 1993.

Oskison, John Milton. *The Singing Bird*. Norman: University of Oklahoma Press, 2007.

Acknowledgments

I would like to acknowledge the Southern Baptist Historical Library and Archives, Nashville, Tennessee, for the letters of Evan Jones in the Baptist Missionary Magazines, and Bill Sumners, the Director, who sent additional information.

Acknowledgment also to the Oklahoma Historical Society, Oklahoma City, Oklahoma, for the old reclamation documents.

Acknowledgment is due as well to *The Night Has a Naked Soul: Witchraft and Sorcery among the Western Cherokee,* by Alan Kilpatrick, Syracuse University Press, 1997, for fragments of chants used in the book.

Acknowledgment to Oklahoma City University for a first reading from the manuscript, April 13, 2007.

Acknowledgment also to Fred Gomeringer at the Oklahoma Historical Society, who spent several hours finding the reels and folders of microfilm I needed.

Thanks to Daniel Heath Justice for his comments.